Pack Star

Shasta de Leon

Smith Book Investments

ebook ISBN 979-8-9948866-0-1

Paperback ISBN 979-8-9948866-2-5

Book cover illustration by TinaIlustra

Book cover titlework and border by KILLDERA

Chapter heading illustration by TinaIlustra

Paperback formatting by Shasta de Leon

Edit by Storrie Laine Lit

First edition 2026

Dedication

To everyone looking for their well-behaved alpha...

Contents

Preface

Pack Star was first introduced in Mads Vol. 2 A Cash City Omegaverse Story. They were dancers and escorts at the O'Bannon pack house, a seedy, underground den of crime and immoral decay. Omega Aurora O'Bannon, the daughter of the overlord of the pack house Legs O'Bannon, stumbled upon the dangerous truth—five of these beta girls formed a pack.

In this world, betas do not form packs, they are reserved for alphas and omegas, with an occasional beta addition. A pack of five beta women is unheard of. It can be met with disdain and even hostility. They can't bond, since only an alpha bite can bond people together, so their connection is based on love and devotion towards one another. That being said, Pack Star always wanted an omega to center themselves around. Desperate to keep Aurora around, they made an offer, but she refused. Eventually, Aurora bonded with Pack Soto, and everyone is happy about the decision.

Legs O'Bannon was killed by his own kept tiger, succumbing to injuries weeks later in the hospital, and Pack Star moved out of the pack house to the next stage of their life.

I wanted to give my Stars their own story, and their own happy ending. I wanted them to have their cake and eat it, too. This is that story—happy reading!

xxx Shasta

Introduction

The omegaverse is as diverse as the writers who write it. Every author has their own rules when it comes to this speculative fiction world. In mine, the designations do not shift. There are alpha, beta, and omega designations only. Around 80% of the human population is designated beta, while the rest is made up mainly of alphas, with an even smaller population of omegas. Typically, betas do not form packs. Pack Star is unique in this regard. They are not able to bond, since only alphas can create bonds with their bite. If you want to learn more, please visit my **Comprehensive Guide to the Omegaverse** on La Femme Omegaverse Substack. Happy reading—

Profiles

Pack Star

Sauvignon

Our main character for this novella, Sauvignon was known as Legs's favorite escort in the Pack House. She was always at his side and in his bed. Sauvignon kept this position to help deter him from focusing on the other Stars. She is a Black woman, the best dancer, and gold is her favorite color. Scent: Hot cinnamon

Carmen

The pack lead, and second tallest Star. She is a red-headed Latina. She's fearless, fair, and loves her Stars. She's willing to do anything it takes to make sure they're safe. She loves bodysuits, tattoos, and boho accessories. Scent: Cocoa

Honey

She's the tallest, the curviest, and the most sexual Star. She loves to be naked, and her language of love is physical touch. She wears many wigs and very tall shoes. She wants an omega to dote on and love. She may be all sex appeal, but Honey has a way of always seeing things clearly and solving problems with simple solutions. Scent: Honeycomb

Tara

The youngest and most blonde. She is always in everyone's business and knows all the secrets. She just wants to be loved. Tara can be easily intimidated and is a great sexual sub. Scent: Lavender

Lucy

A femme domme who can be known for her icy exterior and cold-hearted decisions. But that's only because she knows what to do to take care of the most vulnerable. Lucy is of Japanese descent and has a French bob haircut. She loves wearing black and anything leather. Scent: Mulberry

Chapter 1

Sepp

His sweaty, strained back is a masterpiece of bends and curves. I let my hands feel the taut muscles as he undulates underneath me, my cock shoved deep into his ass. Quickly, I pull my hand away, afraid it's too intimate. Too tender for this.

But I could enjoy his back. I rub my palm down his spine, and he lets out a primal, sinfully sweet, omega moan, shoving back into me. I have him pressed into his nest materials: an oversized white comforter and cotton pillows.

Monroe loves decorating in white and then being upset when it stains. His nest will be another fucking mess, and I'll have to hear about it. Not that I mind when he's being fussy.

The nest smells like a sweet coconut and lime dream. I'm doing my best not to let it drive me into a rut. Monroe has always smelled good, but now he's in heat, and I fear it's sending me over the edge.

Lightning cracks filling Monroe's nest with harsh light. It's followed by earth shattering thunder. The wind and rain continue to pelt the walls from outside the apartment. But my attention is all on the pretty omega underneath me. He's set the rhythm he needs to satisfy his heat, I am simply a hard cock for him to get off on.

He wants my knot, the enlarged base of my cock, and by shoving his ass so far back, he's getting most of it inside. When I think he's had enough, I unclench my jaw and finally let him have it. I was hoping his actual alphas would arrive before I'd need to knot him.

He's not in his right mind.

We're not supposed to be fucking. I've never fucked him—or anyone—in the eighteen months I've been his handler, but the storm caused his alphas to be late to his heat, and I couldn't handle watching him beg and plead, tears running down his face, shivering with need. I'm only a man, not a machine like so many people think.

I do possess feelings.

It's just hard to tell.

Monroe is still crying into his pillows. I can't stand when he cries. No alpha can handle an omega crying. It's devastating. I look up at the ceiling and pray to god I won't be fired for this, and then with a shout, I come inside my ward's asshole.

"Please, my god. Sepp, please push it in. I want more. Deeper. Harder. Don't stop," he cries. "Show me mercy. Give me your knot. I want your big, fucking knot. I want it so badly, Sepp. Don't deny me. Please. Don't say no."

To ease his fears that I'll deny him my knot, I shove my cock deep into him until his tight hole swallows my entire knot up. It enlarges and traps us together.

"Thank you. Thank you. Thank you," the omega chants. We will see how he truly feels about this when he comes out of it in a few days. His alphas burst into the nest and see us trapped together. Monroe sleeps like a sweet lamb, and I sweat and pant above him.

I hate these guys. Two jackasses. Monroe likes them, but he likes everyone. Sanford is the smaller one. He lets Monroe fuck him. Drew is the big one. He does not let Monroe fuck him.

For an omega, Monroe loves to stick his cock into things.

Maybe that's why my affection for him can only go so far. I wouldn't really like to be topped, I don't think. It doesn't sound appealing. Then again, I hardly ever get close to anyone whom I'd like to fuck.

Anyone but Monroe.

"Fuck. He looks like he needed that," Sanford points out. They remove their clothes and enter the nest. They've been Monroe's alphas for a handful of heats now. Normally an alpha would need permission to enter a nest, but they are all too comfortable.

There's no contract or promise made amongst these people. They aren't a pack. They don't live near each other. But they do go out. Date. Fuck. Hook up. Spend all night singing karaoke and then suck each other off.

It's pretty strange, but while they aren't compatible, they keep falling back into each other.

So they aren't upset I fucked the omega.

Actually, quite the opposite.

"Damn, Sepp, I didn't know you were like that."

I grind my teeth. Drew gets on my nerves, if I'm being honest. My surname is Seppton. Ken Seppton. Monroe started calling me Sepp, and at this point, I'm not sure these guys know my real name.

"He was in need," I explain, my jaw tight and my patience low. "It had gone on too long. We tried the dildo, but you know how he is."

When Monroe wants something, nothing else will do.

"Yeah, we do. That storm is wild out there. I hope you have enough food in the house for us."

Drew treats me like a servant. Sanford isn't much better.

But I'm not a fucking butler. I'm Monroe's handler. He's an un-bonded omega, I'm paid to care for him. Male omegas are rare, and when Monroe's parents died when he was young, my clan took over his care. Clans are large groups of packs and unbonded alphas and omegas. Clan Foxx ensured his safety. For omegas, care doesn't end at 18, but goes until they are bonded.

Monroe is 21 and studies art at the nearby community college. We live together in this apartment. I go to all his classes. I go shopping for him. I make most of the meals. I arrange the housekeeping. I even manage his heat.

Hence why these guys are here. Monroe liked them, so we've kept them around.

He doesn't usually go for alphas.

He likes betas. Beta girls, to be exact.

The problem is, he's kind of shy around girls. Insanely shy. And most beta girls don't understand his omega charm. They think he's too slight, too pretty, and way too sweet.

Alphas are easier, he says. Not like beta women, who are every-thing.

Sauvignon

My pack of beta girls, Pack Star, lounge around our loft apartment in the early afternoon, enjoying a day where we are all together. Honey is spread out on the beanbag chair wearing nothing but her good looks. Her beautiful breasts are being used as a pillow by Tara. They are chatting and playing games on their phones. Lucy is sitting on a stool next to the kitchen sink, cutting up an apple. And Carmen is busy scuffing up the bottoms of her new 9-inch pleaser shoes she'll wear when she dances next at the club.

Carmen is my best friend, and she can't keep still. Her energy is harnessed in doing our nails, running the dishes, giving us new piercings, or organizing her collections of things she insists she doesn't have.

We are all on shift tonight at the strip club, except Carmen. It's rare to be on the same shift, but we got four out of five working tonight. I don't dance anymore. I bartend or take cash at the door. Ever since Legs O'Bannon, our pimp, got eaten by that tiger, I just can't get myself back on stage.

The five of us were dancers and escorts at a pack house. The O'Bannon pack house. I was Legs's favorite escort. I'd guessed we were dating if I ever wanted to give it a name. Carmen and Legs also messed around. She would mess around with his daughter, too, so she's got some issues to work out. Actually, most of the Stars messed around with Aurora O'Bannon. She was an omega and sent them into a frenzy.

My pack of beta girls love omegas. They all want one for our pack.

Carmen is our leader. She's brilliant and protective. Her halo of red hair frames her serious, matriarchal face.

Honey is our most outgoing. She's tall and curvy with light brown skin and enough wigs to always keep men guessing.

Tara is a busy body. She's small and blonde, with big blue eyes that want to see everything.

Lucy works in the shadows. She just cut her hair into a black French bob and looks like a secret agent with freckles.

And I'm the broken one.

I shielded the Stars from most of our old boss's evil tendencies. Maybe a little too much because they all had this insane fantasy of bonding with Aurora.

Legs was a monster. He viewed women, especially betas, as lesser beings. He'd collar us, subject us to his cruel fantasies, withhold our money, and make us chase simple conditions like food, friendship, and entertainment. Until he died, we'd been saving money to buy ourselves out of his service. It was going to be astronomical.

"Oh my god, look how cute Collette is!" Honey turns her phone screen to show a social media post of Aurora with her new bunny, Collette. Aurora liked us well enough. She loved screwing around behind her dad's back, but she didn't love us.

She loved Locke Soto.

And now she's with him. I'd feel bad for her because Locke has another omega, Cadi, but they ended up falling in love, too. Their pack is huge. Two omegas—unheard of. One beta. Three alphas. In total, Pack Soto has two women and four men.

Because their pack has alphas, they can actually bond. My pack, Pack Star, is five beta girls. We can't actually bond, since alphas have that special ability to bite and bond people together. It feels like we are bonded, though. I always know what these girls are thinking and feeling. We share a bed. We share money and clothes. We share everything.

So, they all know I'm depressed as hell.

They don't know what to do about it though. Carmen has been urging me to agree to see a therapist. I'll go. I'll go. One day. I don't want to tell someone I'm sad that Legs, a guy I didn't even like, died. I don't know. Sounds like something I should already be over.

And yet...I feel like a great fog is always surrounding me.

When I'm not working at the strip club, Flash House, I'm sleeping. My head hurts while I'm awake. I can't remember the last time something was interesting.

I'm just processing the last year of my life in that pack house from hell.

"Aurora is going to hair school. Maybe we should, too. We could start our own salon," Honey muses to herself.

"Honey, that's actually a great idea," Carmen says. She sets her cigarette into a brass ashtray, done with it.

"What did I say?" Honey asks, genuinely not knowing what she said. I crack a rare smile. Honey is always full of brilliant ideas, told so casually she doesn't even notice.

"Then we can't dance anymore," Tara protests.

"I don't know what I'd do at a salon," Lucy says as she stabs a piece of apple off a plate and brings it up to her mouth and takes a small bite.

"You could use it as a front for your real business—killing off dirty husbands at the bequest of their wives!" Honey again with the brilliant ideas.

Lucy turns to her with her mouth open.

"Honey," Carmen chides.

"What, what did I say?"

Again, I smile, but it fades quickly. I love my Stars with all my heart. I'd follow them anywhere. If they want to get cosmetology licenses and start a salon, I'd do it. Carmen would run it. She has a great head for business and leadership. I'm looking at her now as she's busy thinking. She knows it's a great idea.

I don't know if I'd like it. I don't want to go to school. But I would go if they did.

Honey sighs wistfully and resumes looking at Aurora's social feed. She misses her. Honey wasn't even the one who pushed for us to ask Aurora to be our omega. Honey and Aurora messed around the most. Then it was Aurora and Carmen who were always going at it. Aurora scared Tara to death, but most people do. She's easily spooked. Despite that, she wanted Aurora intensely.

But it was Lucy who put us up to the idea. Lucy and Aurora hardly interacted. One day, long after we were rejected and no longer living at the pack house, as I washed Lucy's hair in the shower, she told me. She said that we would all love to take care of a sweet omega. It would balance us out. She also said we should consider letting an alpha in, so we could be bonded for real.

An alpha.

No way.

The image of Legs O'Bannon with his shiny teeth comes into my mind, and I shiver. All alphas do is take, take, take, take...

"Hey Sauvignon," Carmen says as she stands above me, dressed only in G-string panties and a fringed silk kimono we thrifted together last year. "I don't want to go to The Pinched Rose tonight. Can you cover for me?"

The Pinched Rose is a sex shop open late at night. Carmen often picks up the 7pm-3am shift. It pays well, and it's easy work. Plus, there's an entire section of clothing that we get an employee discount on. I'm supposed to be at the Flash House tonight with everyone else.

"Won't the club..."

"I want to dance tonight. It's a full moon. The tips are going to be killer, I can tell. Please?"

I could never deny her. She's my best friend. Plus, I wouldn't dance on my shift. I'd just work the bar. Everyone there dances during their shift, except the manager and security. So, whether you tend bar, take orders, or clean the private rooms between sessions, you also get on stage once or twice an hour.

Except me. I have a special pass to just bar tend. If Carmen takes my shift, she gets stage time. We pool our tips, so having four of us dancing at the club is better than three.

"Of course. You can count on me."

I look over in time to see Tara and Honey on the beanbag chair getting into a more friendly position. Carmen tracks my gaze to them as well. Tara kneels between Honey's legs, teasing her and kissing along her inner thighs. Honey got some tanning lotion that smells like coconut, and it's been driving her crazy.

Lucy stops stabbing her fruit, her knife hovering mid air, and watches.

The tone in the air shifts. The glass windows looking out into this skyline of this port city might as well fog up. Tara loves eating pussy. And ass. More so than any one of us. And Honey...she has a great cunt. I don't blame her for constantly trying to seduce her pack mate.

Carmen sinks down into the cushions with me. Her body pressed against me and I lean back.

If sexuality were a spectrum, I'd be the most straight member of Pack Star, but that's not saying much. I always imagined myself with a man as a partner, but not so much anymore, not after Legs...

Tara's kisses make it to Honey's center. She spreads her legs wide on the edges of the beanbag, and Tara reaches up and grabs her thick thighs before pressing her tongue to her center. Honey moans, and so does Carmen next to me.

I wish I wasn't depressed as hell. Maybe this would make me wet. Instead, it makes me feel the presence of the dark cloud even more than usual. I'm empty, and this proves it.

I still do them the service of watching, while Tara undulates and devours Honey. They are beautiful. There's no denying it.

Honey is close, and Tara doesn't stop. Honey's legs curl over her shoulders and Tara's fingers enter her, leading her further and further over the edge.

We all watch with rapt interest as Honey comes apart. Her voice rings out like church bells. Tara climbs up, and they make out and snuggle into the chair.

Carmen stands up.

"Well, I'm going to find my vibrator," she announces.

Lucy follows after her to our bedroom with a little bounce in her step.

I pull my knees up to my chin and just watch how sweet my Stars are together. I love the aftercare. The touching and sweet compliments. How both people share how they feel and talk about what they both just did together. I wish I knew that kind of intimacy. I wonder if I'll be able to love again.

Chapter 2

Sepp

A few days after Monroe's heat is over, all hell breaks loose. It comes as no surprise since I could feel it in the air when his heat ended; He wouldn't talk to me, and when he'd look at me, it was with cold eyes.

It's just gotten worse as time goes on.

Monroe is mad at me.

Probably because we fucked, and we fucked when he was going into heat, so he was half out of his mind. I tried to apologize, but he threw toast at me. Toast I had just made for him. Then he ran into his room and slammed the door.

Omegas can be very dramatic.

He also has been snippy with his two alpha friends, Drew and Sanford. They are here now and everyone is yelling. The guys came over to play video games and fool around, as is the custom for Saturday nights, but Monroe has started yelling.

I don't want to get in the way, so I've been in my bedroom for the last hour hearing their muffled fight through the walls.

I'm not going to deny that I don't hope, secretly, he's finally done with the alphas. I'm not saying I wish he'd turn his attention to me—though the thought of that happening stops my breath—I just think he deserves so much more. He should go out with a girl or two as well. Monroe is smaller than most men and has an angelic face with a devastating smile. He's in great shape. He has black hair that has perfectly smooth strands hanging in his face, shaved on the sides, a perfect texture for touching.

...and those baby blue eyes...

I groan and put my head between my knees.

That's when I notice how there's no more yelling. But, there is loud pounding. Oh my god, are they fucking?

I leave my room and drift down the hall, but the pounding isn't from sex and bodies, it's from something hitting the inside of his bedroom door.

I open Monroe's door just in time for a flying green dildo to hit me in the chest. It bounces off and onto the carpet next to other similar items that I recognize, and some I don't.

Monroe is in his room throwing dildos and fake pussy sex toys at the door. He is undeterred by my presence.

The pile grows.

And so does his scent. Coconut fills the room, telling me this omega is angry.

"Monroe!" I say sternly. "What happened?"

He keeps flinging his toys. He has to run out soon. Tears wet his cheeks, and he shows off all his sharp, omega teeth in a grimace. I realize he will not stop. So I take three giant strides over to him and grab the big black dildo out of his hand, and then grab his shoulder.

"Stop! What is going on?" I shake him a little and it seems to snap him out of it. I don't want to manhandle him too much, because of my size.

"Why don't you..." His forehead crashes into my chest.

"Did something happen with your friends?"

"They aren't my friends!" He turns and rubs his cheek into my shirt.

"Did something happen with Drew and Sanford?" I ask with a softer tone.

"I just don't like them anymore. I don't like their smells. I hate the sound of them laughing. Sanford has dirty fingernails. Did you notice?"

I actually did.

"Will you hold me, please?" he asks with a shaky voice.

I move my arms to hold him tight against me. I don't even think about how I probably shouldn't. Ever since his heat I've been scheming how to get him in my arms again...knowing full well I shouldn't. He's always been touchy with me: cuddling next to me on the couch, leaning into me in public, sleeping on my shoulder in cars, but I don't do it back.

"So, what happened?"

His energy is so chaotic. I'm trying my best to let him take my calming energy from me. *Feel calm in my arms, please, Monroe.*

"I snapped at them because they were annoying the hell out of me! They come over and eat my food. They play my games. And now they smell bad! I was pissed. And..." he takes a deep breath, "I know how belittling they can be to you. I broke up with them."

I hold him tighter.

"I'm sorry."

"It's fine. It's ok."

I look at the mess he's made with the multi-colored pile of silicon phallic and yonic toys.

"What's up with the sex toys?"

He looks over at it, too.

"Oh, I want nothing we used together."

I try not to chuckle. The way he says it is so sincere and sweet. Without thinking, I kiss him atop his head. He goes completely still.

I clear my throat.

"Let me go get a bag. I'll toss them."

My lips tingle.

"I may need some new ones sooner rather than later."

It's then that I smell his scent change. He's turned on. My mouth waters. That's my cue to get going. We move apart.

"It's going to be ok, Monroe. We will find you someone new."

His jaw ticks.

What I wouldn't give to hear what he's thinking. Who does he want now that he doesn't have his alphas? Does he have someone in mind?

It's later that I find myself in the dark throwing two trash bags full of sex toys into a dumpster when I get a text. Monroe says, "Can you please bring some new ones back. Please." And sends some questionable emojis. Crying. Hearts. Praying hands.

As his handler, I often do his shopping for him, especially when he's incapacitated. He's not exactly incapacitated, but I did leave him eating sherbet from a carton and watching old romance movies from the 90s, so never mind. The guy is in it.

I wish I could comfort him.

Like how an alpha comforts an omega.

My mouth on his cock. Switching to my hand so I can tell him how beautiful I find him. Shove my finger into his slick ass. Omegas slick their asses—something I was trying not to enjoy so much when I helped him with his heat.

I look up at our apartment. The light dances on the ceiling from the tv. Some of his paintings hang on the wall behind him. It's not right for someone in my position to take advantage of their omega ward.

There's no way out of it. Monroe can't be mine.

I text him back and tell him to give me a list, then I get into my car and drive to the only sex shop I can remember. The moon is full and shines in the sky just above it, like a beacon.

The Pinched Rose.

It's midnight. What a time to be going to a sex shop. The parking lot is empty. My phone pings with Monroe's list. My ears ring and my heart seizes.

It's all fake pussies. No cocks.

Why does it feel like Monroe isn't done being angry?

Chapter 3

Sauvignon

I'm watching the group chat like I'm in the fucking cuck chair of my pack's super fun night at Flash House.

It's a full moon. A Saturday night. Carmen has new pleasers. They keep sending videos and photos: flashing their cash, making out, showing off all the attractive customers. It's so unfair.

There are never attractive men there while I'm working.

The Pinched Rose is your average skanky sex shop. It's its own building in the parking lot of an abandoned department store. There's supposed to be an armed guard here with me, but Carter is often a no show, like tonight.

Customers walk through the metal detectors, and then hand me their ID while I sit in this elevated tower. I scan their ID and keep it with me until they leave. If they have purses or bags, I have to take them too.

Other than that, I can descend the spiral staircase from my tower and help them shop, or wait for them at the check-out counter. Many people like getting help with shopping. There are naturally a lot of questions.

It is a sex shop, and I'm here to help.

I mostly get beta couples or omegas that shop here. Especially at night. Alphas aren't really into toys. Thankfully. Which is what I keep thinking about when a lone alpha comes through the vestibule and waits for me to take his ID.

I haven't had a customer in over an hour.

And this one makes my brain short circuit.

He's tall, like most alphas, but also just absolutely huge. His top half is that insane inverted triangle shape that would make any girl weak in the knees.

I shrink back, hoping to be less visible. He has a gorgeous face, in a way that makes me wonder if he would also think I'm beautiful. He's clean shaven with dark brown hair that's cut very well. His kind eyes find mine.

"Hello, are you...open?"

I'm just staring at him from the far side of my tower. The gate is closed, so he can't enter the shop until I press a button for it to open.

Wow, his voice is so low and warm.

"Uh, yeah, we're open."

I take a shallow breath, hoping any oxygen will help my anxiety.

He smiles a little at my shocked face and reaches up, sliding his ID across the shelf in my tower.

My nails are long with gems and glitter painted into the gel, his eyes go to the shimmer. Before I scan his ID in, I read the name—Ken Seppton. 34 years old. Alpha. Libra.

It doesn't say Libra, but I do the math.

I'm an Aquarius. Compatible signs.

"You taking my information?" the man below me asks teasingly. I smile, scan the ID, then open the gate.

"Let me know if you need any help," I say on instinct.

Calling my bluff, the alpha says, "I'd love some help, actually."

My heart races. I haven't spent time, one-on-one, with an alpha since Legs. He was tall too, but skinny as a sapling. Ken here is like a bear on its hind legs.

"Sure, yeah..."

Get it together, Sauvignon! It's just a man!

I honestly can't tell if my anxiety is because I'm scared of him or attracted. Maybe it's both. When was the last time anything made my heart race?

I'm wearing five-inch gold pumps and a matching gold mini dress. It works well against my warm brown skin. I haven't been doing much to my hair lately, but earlier this week I thought I was going to be at the club more, so I'd gotten a blowout. It bounces as I walk down the tower towards the noble knight.

He looks like a warrior. I wonder if he needs a queen?

What has gotten into me?!

Once I am standing on the same level as him, I see why I was intimidated. He'd snap Legs in two. He's all mass. And he smells incredible. Like apricots in the warm sun. There's honey there too. Apricots and honey.

"Hi," his voice still has that warm resonance, but there's a softness to it.

"Hello, welcome in. I'm Sauvignon. What are you shopping for today?"

His cheeks go pink at my question. It's so charming I can't help but smile. He looks up something on his phone and then reads off some things...

"Intergalactic male masturbator, stamina training stroker, a male masturbator with...wings, fae-tastic fleshlight, water massager play box...oh, and a super soft cock sheath."

He looks up at me, his face is now completely red.

"I'm sorry."

"It's fine," I tell him truthfully. "I can certainly help you. Is this for solo play or with a partner?"

His hand goes to the back of his neck.

"Oh no. It's for my omega. I mean, it's for an omega. I'm his handler. He's asked me to get him some things."

I step up closer to the man and put my hand on him to show him it's fine. We get handlers in here sometimes. Omegas are needy. I know that. He and I both look at my hand on his arm.

All alone and touching alphas, look at how brave I am.

"Is that the complete list?"

"There are a few more things. God, I'm sorry, but I have to tell you that you look beautiful in that dress. I've been thinking about it for the last few minutes, and I just had to tell you."

His compliment warms me from the inside out. I've been in these kinds of spaces for years, having men pant after me, and the way he worded that was so sincere and complimentary. He didn't tell me he thinks I'm beautiful, or that he'd like to have sex with me. He said I look beautiful in my dress. Something I picked out and washed, and cared for. Something I spent so much time and energy on.

"Thank you, Ken."

His face pinches.

"What? Is that not your name?"

"Sorry, my omega...the omega I care for, Monroe, calls me Sepp and I've gotten used to it. Call me Sepp."

This is the second time he claimed him as his and then corrected himself. My senses tell me there's something there between him and his omega. Handlers aren't supposed to be forming intimate relationships with their wards, but who am I to tell someone who they can and cannot love?

"Sounds like your omega is in need of some serious cock stimulation."

Sepp grimaces.

"He just separated from his alphas. He's kind of upset, actually."

"Which is why he's got his handler out after midnight at a sex shop!"

He chuckles. My hand is still on his arm. It's so warm. I enjoy being close, the apricot smell is lovely.

"You get it. Am I not the first handler here looking for cock warmers for a male omega crying into a tub of sherbet?"

"Apricot sherbet?" I ask with a laugh.

His face falls, and he takes a step away from me, looking anywhere but me. Oh no, I messed up. Why did I say that? That's so fucking rude.

He clears his throat.

"You know, actually, if you could just point me in the right direction, I could probably figure it out."

"I'm sorry," I rush to say. He turns completely away from me. "I don't know why I said that. Let me help you. I'll behave, I swear."

He considers it and then nods his head.

"Ok, follow me. We have all those things in a few sections. Does your omega like bright colors?"

He is distant as he replies that Monroe does like bright colors. I feel so bad that I teased him, my mood also shifts. What am I even doing? I got excited and flirty, and landed face first. I should have kept things more professional.

The thing is, I haven't been able to orgasm since Legs died.

I've tried on my own. With Lucy. With Carmen. My clit sucker just whirls and whirls until I give up. Even if I were to decide that this mountain of a man was worthy of a hookup, he'd probably not be able to get me there.

We arrive at the far corner of the shop, where the overhead lights are missing so it's kind of dark. Which is fitting.

"Here are the cock sleeves. He said he wanted a soft one? These pink ones are much softer than the clear. If he's into bright colors, this would work."

"Your voice has changed," Sepp says instead of looking at the display.

I open and close my mouth. I was trying to be more chill. Guess I took a nosedive.

Sepp gets a little closer, bowing his head.

"Can I tell you a secret?"

In this dark corner of my sex shop, with no one around, it feels like the perfect place for a secret.

I nod my head.

"I do...like my omega ward, Monroe. I like him a lot."

My shoulders ease down, and I step even closer, wanting to hear his deep, whispering reverberations more.

"He's really great. He's shy and funny. I like when he's fussy or ridiculous." Oh, boy! What a secret. I try my best not to show how excited this is making me. "There's a big size difference between us. He's small and pretty, and I'm a giant. It's sexy. Like he'll cuddle me on the couch sometimes and he's like a little rabbit and I'm...I don't know."

"You're in love with your omega?" I ask.

He nods slowly.

"I am."

"Does he love you back?"

This he takes a long time to think about.

"I don't know. But I do think he's mad at me."

Fuck me. Size difference? Unrequited love? Yearning? This is too good. Where's my phone? I have to tell my pack. They'll flip out.

I take a deep breath and focus on the man in front of me. He just looks so stressed, like he's really struggling. What would that be like? To be in love with someone you had to be with all day and night? There's no way the omega doesn't see his affection for him. Omegas are sensitive. They are possessive, too. They don't hold back on letting people know what they think or feel about something, even if they don't use their words.

"Do you think this list he gave you was some sort of message?"

Sepp nods his head.

"I do, but I can't figure it out."

"Let's figure it out then."

Sepp smiles wide. "You'll help me?"

"Of course! I mean, I know a thing or two about forming a pack. And sex. So you are in good hands."

"You're bonded?"

I scoff and look at him like he's insane.

"I said I'm in a pack, not that I'm bonded. There's five of us, all beta women. So, bonding isn't in our inventory right now."

Only alphas can bond people into a pack. Something about the enzymes in their saliva and the bite they have. Betas and omegas can't mark someone like that. It's really rather unfortunate since alphas are often so overbearing.

"Are you looking for an alpha?" he asks so quickly that by the time it comes out he looks horrified.

It's not a wrong question, and we've been asked it before. I think for the longest time the idea of having a man, of any designation, was so truly off the table. When you have a man controlling your life for as long as we did, constantly testing our safety and self worth, it's hard to open that part of you again.

"I'm sorry, that's none of my business."

"No, it's fine. We are looking for an *omega*, actually." I typically wouldn't tell a stranger this, but I feel comfortable around him. "Lucy, my pack mate, mentioned maybe allowing an alpha in, a well-behaved one."

I'm not sure they come well-behaved. If I'm being honest.

I watch him try to ask his next question but come up blank, and I also watch the way he looks down at my body and my hips, with admiration and heat. I yank the pink cock sleeve off the display, push it into his chest until he takes it, then I walk away, leading him to another section.

Maybe I'll test him to see how good a boy he can be. My pussy is telling me he'd make a very good boy, indeed. But I need to make sure.

A curiosity warms my insides up.

Can this man make me come?

Over my shoulder, I ask, "Does Monroe like things that vibrate?"

Chapter 4

Sepp

She's a beautiful woman, in the kind of way that makes me hope she finds me tolerable. Everything about her is stunning. Her glittery legs. Her gold dress that fits her like it were made for her. Those shoes that she balances so delicately on. She has red-tinted lips that I hope would transfer if she were to ever put them on someone. Someone. Me.

I'm having trouble breathing.

Her eyes are her best feature, and I'm not being an asshole for saying that. They are soulful. Like she's lived a thousand lives. It makes me want to know what she's been through.

She takes me to the masturbators. She asked me something, but I'm not entirely sure what it was. Once we stand in front of them, she asks again.

"Does your omega like things that vibrate?"

"Oh...I don't know." I think back to the pile of toys. Most of them were inert, non-mechanical.

I'm about to tell her, but she's got a little purple stick out of a package and turns it on. The buzzing sound sends my thoughts flying.

She asked if my omega liked vibrations, not me. I'm not even sure how I'd answer at this point. Probably how I'd like anything being held by her long, beautiful fingers. I'm not even looking at the stick, I'm mesmerized by her fingernails. How do they get so many gems onto such a small space? Do they fall off?

She touches the tip of the vibrating stick to my nose. Like a snake being charmed, I remain still, looking past the stick to her amber-colored eyes.

"Sepp?"

"Yeah?"

"Did you hear me?"

"Hm?"

Her red lips spread into a clever smile.

"How does this feel?" she asks like it's not the first time. I slowly reach up and hold her wrist, pulling the toy off my nose, not breaking eye contact.

"I don't think that's where this goes."

A gorgeous pink color rises underneath her cheeks.

"It can go lots of places."

"Like where?"

"Well, if it's for a couple, one partner might use it on the other's clit or insert it inside."

It's not lost on me that suddenly a woman's body parts are being discussed. Is she cleverly putting that image into my mind? It's got me thinking that tonight, during this full moon, inside this empty sex shop, something more may be happening here.

As an alpha, I have a keen sense of smell, so I can smell when Sauvignon is turned on. Earlier, when she touched my arm with her icy hand, and now, as I hold her wrist. She's joyously responsive. How would she react if I laid my body over hers, touching every inch of her, warming her up entirely?

Despite my train of thoughts, I let her wrist go, one finger at a time, until she's free.

She turns back to the display.

"Your omega listed a few things that recreate the feel of someone fucking someone else. Do you think what he is trying to say is that he wants to fuck you?"

I sigh heavily, shaking my head.

"When we were together...the one time," I admit, "It was me who was doing the fucking."

She's not startled by this information, instead, she thinks. Her fingers tap her chin, and she gets a perfect pout on her lips.

Sauvignon looks through the items a few times, then says, "Does he want you to think about what it felt like when you fucked him, and that's why he chose those things?"

I didn't think about that, but maybe. These are a little different from his usual toys. No thick dildos were even on the list.

"I could see that being the message."

"Well, I don't see any path forward except trying one of these out! How about the Masturbator Megacock30000 that has temperature control? It warms your cock as you fuck it?"

"Yeah, I mean, heat sounds good...wait! Try it out? What do you mean?!"

She said it so casually I didn't even notice how insane that is! We aren't at an Apple Store! What does she mean, try it out?!

"There's a changing room."

"Is this a service you offer?"

"No! Are you kidding me? I'd probably get fired. And they'd call the police."

"Then what're you saying?!"

"I'm only offering because you're a well-behaved alpha, right? You need to know before you go back to Monroe—that's his name, right? Monroe—You need to know if he's sending you a message."

My teeth click shut.

I *am* a well-behaved alpha.

And I know when a beautiful woman is hitting on me. What I don't know is how far she's willing to take this. I'll call her bluff.

"That's right," I drawl. "You agreed to help me. So, is that the one you think we ought to try out?"

She looks down at her hands, holding the flame red cock warming and vibrating masturbator machine shaped like something from an old science fiction movie.

"Yeah. This is the one. Follow me."

I follow behind her, like an obedient dog, watching her ass sway and her back exposed in her dress. What I wouldn't give to run my fingers over her spine while I fuck her from behind...

Fuck me.

She takes me through a second room full of racks of clothes. Lingerie. Sequined bras. Body suits. Cat suits. Latex and BDSM outfits. Then to a purple fur covered door she has to use a key to open.

We enter the room, and it's indeed small. There's a couch and a mirrored ceiling with a leopard print rug on the floor. It's dark and takes a second for my eyes to adjust.

"This is our changing room, though we rarely have it open since people tend to fuck in here, and as the owner says, do nothing the tax man would need to be aware of."

I wonder how far she's going to take this whole thing. Does she do this often? What am I walking into? I just needed to pick up some things for Monroe and now I'm thinking about what this woman's breasts would feel like pressed into my face as I rutted into her warm, wet cunt.

Sauvignon shuts the door and then turns the deadbolt into the jam.

Oh my god, she's serious.

She kneels down in front of a coffee table that's against the far wall, her back turned to me, and unpackages the device.

I steel my nerves and go over to the overstuffed black vinyl couch and sit in the middle, spreading my legs wide and waiting patiently. She's going to start laughing soon, then this will all be more or less a silly prank.

I decide now, that no matter what happens next, I'm going to ask her out.

Once the device is out of the package, she wipes it down with some cleaning wipes, then, when she's satisfied, she crawls across the rug towards me, kneeling between my legs.

"Have you ever used this before?"

I'm not sure I'm able to speak. Seeing her from this angle is almost too much. So I shake my head just once.

"Me neither. But I read the instructions. Seems easy enough."

She places her elbow on my knee, then shows me how it works. I stop her with my hand on hers.

"Sauvignon. Are we just messing around? What're we doing here?"

All her flirty humor drains out of her face.

"We're just having fun."

"Do you really mean for me to take my cock out and fuck this thing in front of you?"

Her pupils blow wide. Her lips part, and I wait as she weighs her response. Inside this dark room, where all I can hear is her heartbeat and our breaths, it feels like we are in our own dream world.

"If you wanted, I think I'd be ok with that," she whispers.

"What if I touched you while I used it? Would you be ok with that?"

"You'd want to?"

"Yes."

"Do you do this with all your late night customers?" I ask. Not that I'm going to judge her, I just need to know the situation here.

She swallows, then shakes her head.

"I've had a hard time lately, and being around you, talking with you, has been really nice. It's the full moon, and..."

"You're so fucking beautiful," I cut her off. Satisfied enough to dive in headfirst. "I don't think I've ever met a more beautiful woman. I'm resisting the urge to throw you over my shoulder and take you away. I'm so fucking drawn to you." I place my hand on her face, stroking her jaw with my thumb. "Can I kiss you?"

She closes her eyes and sits up closer, so I take the hint and move down on her lips. They are more amazing than I had imagined. Pillow soft, and they fit perfectly against me. I take the device from her hands and drop it to the side, pulling her closer to me with my hand on her back. She moans and I take her deeper, sliding my tongue against hers.

"Oh my god," she sighs into my mouth, and I smell how turned on she is. It's absolutely delicious. I pick her up and place her in my lap, her knees slide down either side of me. As I kiss her, I push her lower back into me over and over again, encouraging the rocking movement. Each time she rocks into me, she gets wetter and wetter.

"I don't think," I say over her mouth, continuing to push her into me over and over again, so she can feel my cock between our bodies getting harder and harder. "I want to fuck the machine. I'd rather feel the real thing."

"But your omega..."

"You know what my omega really wants?"

I kiss her neck and get her to bend back so I can suck on her nipple through her gold dress.

"What?" she asks breathlessly.

I don't answer her, not yet. I want to take her for myself right now. I work her nipple and continue to rock her hips into me. I'm a very big man, and if I do get to fuck her, she's going to need to be nice and ready.

Monroe wants beta women.

That's what the omega wants.

I see him wistfully watching them pass by. I see the porn he watches on his computer—*Beta Girls Dominate Male Omega*. I've been around when he's tried to hit on them and failed miserably.

I wonder if this is fate.

Five beta women looking for an omega. Would they want a male omega? Are all of them into men or just Sauvignon? And if they chose him, and me, maybe I could have it all...No, I can't do this. I'm Monroe's handler, not his alpha!

Sauvignon moans, and my head turns into goo.

I pick her up and spin us until she lies across the couch on her back.

"Can I taste you?" Her smell is driving me absolutely insane.

"Please, yes! Sepp, I want you."

I slide down her body, kissing her over her beautiful dress, then I get to her center. I slowly bunch up the material, revealing the top of her pantyhose. She's not wearing underwear underneath, so behind the glimmer gold sheer material, I see her dark curls. I want to die. It's the hottest image I've ever seen. I put my mouth on her there, right over the pantyhose and her curls.

Fuck.

There's something about this woman that makes me feel like I have finally found what I've been looking for. My fingers curl over the top of her pantyhose and I inch them down over her hips.

"Rip them off, Sepp. I can't wait."

Absolutely not. Does she think I haven't heard an omega beg for me many times in the last year and a half? I am patient, if nothing else.

I stroke her leg down to her ankle and then take my goddamned time removing one shoe then the other, kissing her ankles and feet. When I'm done, I ease her pantyhose down and off her legs.

"Your legs are a work of art."

She's squirming and panting. It's so beautiful.

When she hears the buzzing sound of a little vibrator, she sits up on her elbows, eyes as wide as dinner plates.

"Sepp!"

I'd taken the little purple stick without her knowing it. With it on, I show her and she goes from shocked to impressed pretty damned fast. I tease her inner thighs with it, and she lays back down with a moan.

"Is the beautiful beta woman in need of an orgasm? I bet she's been hoping and praying all night that a handsome alpha would walk through those doors and use some of these toys on her own aching pussy."

She whines but stops as I ease the vibrating stick between her pussy lips. I stop, then use my fingers to spread her lips wide, using my body to spread her legs wider at the same time.

Then I insert the stick into her cunt, gliding it on her walls, watching her intently until I make contact with that part of her that will make her sing.

I move it in and out, then finally she shouts and grabs at the couch.

"That's it, doll, that's it." I pull it out and then lick her wet cunt, tasting the nectar of someone I will never let go. She's mine after she comes. I move up to her clit and suck it and everything around it into my mouth, hard, then ease the stick back inside, going right to her G spot. Her hands go into my hair and her long sharp nails pierce my scalp. The pain is so damned good.

I don't let up until her orgasm rips through her.

"Sepp! My god!" she screams.

I turn off the stick and toss it to the side.

"Fuck, fuck," she chants, and her legs snap together. I curl over her, holding her close through the aftershocks.

"It's good. It's so good."

I stroke her arms, and a purr breaks out of my chest. I lay over her, with my knees on the ground, easing her back into reality.

My woman.

Mine.

She's mine.

I just need to figure out how to keep her and Monroe.

Chapter 5

Sepp

She turns in my arms, and her lips find mine easily. She kisses me appreciatively and then seductively, and I match her fervor.

My dick is so hard in my pants, but the pain is working for me. I stroke her perfect body, getting more and more worked up. When it's almost too much to bear, I push my cock into the couch for relief.

She breaks away from the kiss to gasp and say, "Do you want to fuck me?"

The world could be ending outside this room, and I wouldn't care. That's where my thoughts are at.

"Yes. You'd really want that?"

I'm an alpha so I have extra anatomy down there. Beta girls are sometimes turned off by it. I pray she knows what she's asking for.

She nods enthusiastically.

"I don't have a condom," I say and look down at the tent in my pants. Not that alphas use condoms. We don't have a tendency to carry venereal diseases, but more than that our knot, a bulbous muscle at the base of our cocks, makes a condom hard to stay on.

"Are you clean? I'm clean."

"I went to the clinic after Monroe's heat. I'm clean."

"Then fuck me with your alpha cock, Sepp. Now."

Fuck yes. Oh my god. I gaze at her lips, not believing she's asking me for this. I know what position I want her in, but I don't want to force her to do something she wouldn't like.

"How do you want me," I ask, and her face goes so soft.

"You really are such a well-behaved alpha." Her hands stroke my face, and a purr breaks out in my chest. I love that she calls me that. "Sepp, put me where you want me."

I run my hand between her legs and make sure she's still wet for me. I can't help but stroke her back and forth between her lips and over her clit.

"Are you sure, doll?"

"Yes."

"I want you on your knees. I want to take you from behind."

"Oh."

I know it's not the most intimate position. Sometimes girls feel like I don't want to see their face while we fuck. I'm not inexperienced, so I've learned a thing or two about how my partner feels about sexual positions.

Sauvignon's mind is no longer here with us, so I wonder if she thinks the same thing. Sauvignon is craving intimacy. Not just fucking. It's why she pets my face and asks me so many questions. If she just wanted my cock, I'd get a different version of her.

"I love your back," I admit. "When you turned around, and I saw your back exposed in this fucking sexy gold dress, I nearly fell to my knees, doll. I've been dreaming of stroking your back while I fuck you. We don't have to do that. I'll sit on the couch while you ride me, if that's what you want."

"No. You can stroke my back. Just don't hit me or slap me."

I stop my hand on her pussy.

She was worried I would slap her ass while I fuck her from behind. My girl does not like degrading herself during sex. Got it. She likes to be worshipped.

"Oh, doll. I will treat you like the work of art you are. Now turn around and stick your ass in the air for your well-behaved alpha."

She sighs with pleasure, and I move away, allowing her to do what I told her. I'll take good care of you, Sauvignon. You don't have to worry about me.

God, she's beautiful.

She is down on her elbows, resting her head on her forearms, and her ass is straight in the air. I love the round shape of her ass, and I make that known by touching her body and moaning. I stand up and take off my pants, then get on the couch behind her. Everything I do to her, she reacts so well to. I touch her dress, she moans. I check her pussy, she shouts fuck. I could tease her for hours, but instead, I line my cock up to her entrance, and push ever so slightly in.

"Oh my god, Sepp! Please. Yes. Fuck me. I want it so badly."

"Me too, doll, me too."

I test her hips for the right hold, and when I get it, I drive into her.

"You're so fucking tight!" I only get half my cock into her, so I pull out and try again. She screams into the couch.

She's going to ruin her makeup, but I guess she doesn't care. Why does that give me the chills?

I drive into her over and over and over again, getting my cock deeper each time.

Her skin breaks out into a sweat, and that's when I run my hand over her spine. I can't even begin to describe how this makes me feel. It's just something I crave. She's so soft and lovely.

This is it. This is the feeling I've always wanted, and it's with the most beautiful woman in the changing room of a sex shop.

I lean over her and say, with my knot pushing at her entrance, desperately wanting to be warmed by her cunt, "There's no machine in the world that would feel better than you wrapped around my cock."

She can't speak, her noises are incomprehensible. So I pull back and fuck her cunt exactly like she needs. She needed this. My fat cock in her aching pussy. I hold her hips and drive into her, slapping my thighs with her ass. My knot butts at her entrance, and each time, she makes the most delicious sound.

My girl.

She needs this.

She needs me.

I fuck her until I'm so close I need to grit my teeth and then I pull out and finish into my hand. I grab her with my clean hand on my way down, crashing into the couch, and pulling her up so she's no longer inverted. I don't want her to fall on her face.

We are both panting, and she curls into me.

"Fuck."

She kisses my neck and licks my ear. I'm so sensitive and it's so necessary for me to calm down.

"Sauvignon, I can't believe you let me fuck you."

"I don't think you have any idea how much I wanted that."

She sees me holding my hand out with my cum, waiting for the right time to find something to clean it off with, and before I can stop her, she's brought my hand up to her mouth and licks my palm.

"Oh fuck!" I groan, and she cleans my hand off with her perfect tongue. "Oh my god, Sauvignon. Oh my god."

I watch in total shock. I knew she was perfect. I knew she was mine.

"So delicious," she says mostly to herself. She leaves my two fingers untouched by her tender tongue. I look up at her face, curious why she's stopped. She sits up and turns towards me, then straddles one of my thighs. I adjust on the couch to give her more room. With my hand up, she directs it down between her legs and puts my two fingers into her wet cunt.

I know who's in charge.

My girl.

"Come on, doll, ride my fingers," I encourage her as she grips the back of the couch.

She's in a total trance as she finds her pleasure with my fingers on her pussy. I move my thumb to her clit and she speeds up, grinding down harder. She's an absolute vision. I'm in awe of this beautiful woman getting off on my cum stained hand.

Mine. Mine. Mine.

She gets closer and closer, and I hold steady, and finally she comes with a shout and her legs clench my arm. I wrap my other arm around her and bring her down into my lap, holding her tight.

"Oh my god, Sepp. Oh my god. That was huge."

"I can tell. Just let go. I've got you."

Chapter 6

Sepp

I'm holding Sauvignon when a buzzing sound rings over the intercom system. She jumps up, out of my arms.

"The door! Someone is here!" She pulls her dress down over her stunning ass. I secretly pout that our time is over, then help her get her shoes on, minus the pantyhose. She runs out of the room as quickly as she can. I shove her pantyhose into my pocket, and gather up the sex toys scattered about.

By the time I get out, I see her talking to a man at the front in a very friendly manner. Jealousy and possession take over my heart, and I try my best to snuff it out.

"Hello! This is Carter, our security guard," she says in a very professional sounding voice.

I nod to the smelly, unkempt man.

"Sorry again, Sauvignon. I was coming off a bender. I hope no one gave you trouble." Carter takes a seat on a tall stool near the gate. He's a beta and very out of shape. I'm surprised they don't have an alpha running security. They are bigger and stronger, with dominant senses. What can Carter do?

"No, of course not, but glad you're here."

Maybe I should stick around. There's no way this man could protect my woman from anything. That gun in its holster has to be just for show. I take my items to the checkout counter and set them down. Sauvignon comes up from the other side and starts ringing me up. She stops at the purple stick, giving me a heated look.

"Yeah, I'm buying that too," I tell her. She smiles, pleased. After she rings me up, I take her hand and put the stick in her palm.

"For you."

She blushes and then hides it away.

"Can I take you out?" I ask.

She hesitates, and a nervous feeling sits in my stomach.

"I don't really date outside of the pack. They'll be happy to hear I slept with someone. I have been really fucked up since an ex. I sort of dated an alpha for a long time, and it wasn't very healthy."

"But your pack is looking for an omega?"

"Yeah."

"Monroe likes beta girls."

She blinks at me.

"Could he meet you all in some way?"

She looks a little confused. But in my mind, a plan is forming. If Monroe and Sauvignon's pack get along, and they want to bond, they'll need an alpha to make it permanent with bite marks. Maybe they'd ask me. I could get Clan Foxx to approve. Possibly. The loophole to being with both Monroe and Sauvignon is becoming more and more clear to me.

"Thursday," she says, taking me out of my scheming. "Most of us will be dancing at the Flash House on Thursday night. Bring him around."

A smile so big that I doubt I've ever felt it before, spreads across my face.

"Thursday. We'll be there. Will I get to see you dance?"

She huffs out a laugh. "Probably not. I'm usually behind the bar. I'll make you a drink."

"It's a date."

She's glowing as she meets me in her tower on the other side of the gate to give me back my ID.

She slides the ID across, it's about eye level. She just looks so much like a princess I can't help it. I hop up, grabbing onto the counter, and pull myself up.

"Hey!" Carter shouts, but I ignore him so I can lean in and kiss the princess. She grabs my face and opens up to me. God, she tastes amazing. I want Monroe to taste her, too.

Hands grab my hips from below and try to pull me down. I leave her lips and let Carter pull me off her.

"Get out of here before I make you!" Carter yells.

"Goodbye, Sauvignon. Until next time!" I shout to her as Carter partially drags me out.

"He's my friend, Carter! Relax!" she says, but Carter still looks stressed.

I smack his shoulder, and he lets me go. I hear her laugh and tell him he's crazy as he gets back into the store.

This is going to work out. I feel it. Good things always start on the night of the full moon.

I crawl into bed minutes after my pack has done the same thing. They were out all night dancing for tips, and I am coming off an all-night shift at the sex shop, and we are all exhausted.

I sigh and wiggle with excitement once I'm deep in the covers and nestled between Carmen and Lucy.

Carmen playfully hits me.

"Stop, Sauvignon, you're too damned wiggly."

I must giggle or something in response because all four of my pack mates sit up in bed and turn to me. Honey is wearing a silk bonnet and pulls off her matching silk eye mask.

"What?" I ask.

"Did you giggle?"

A smile I can't stop spreads across my face.

"She's smiling!" Tara points at my face.

"I can't believe it," Carmen whispers, stunned.

"What happened? Have you finally lost your mind?" Lucy asks sincerely while patting my cheeks.

"No! Stop!" Another giggle comes out of me, and Carmen crashes into me, hugging me close. "It's nothing, I just hooked up with a guy, and he...got me there."

A collective screech rings out in the room from my pack mates. They pile onto me and we all match each other's laughs.

"Tell us everything! How did he do it!" Tara demands.

Once they give me a second to breathe, I tell them about Sepp.

"He was a customer coming in to buy some toys for his omega ward. He's a handler. He wouldn't stop looking at me like he wanted to tear my clothes off and eat me up. He seemed nice. And sweet. So, we went into the changing room and messed around."

"A nice, sweet man!? Impossible!"

"I know! He was also very big. Big hands. Big thighs. Big...cock."

Another round of giggles.

They all know I've been unable to get myself there for months.

"He did this thing where I was in his lap, and he got me to dry hump him, and it got me really close. I was so wet and my pussy was so hot, I could have melted his jeans off. And then he laid me down and used this toy on me, a little purple vibrating stick, while he sucked my clit. I've never felt anything like it. I think I saw god!"

"Fucking hell!"

I pointed to my bag as I described the toy, so Tara gets off the bed to retrieve it.

"This one?" She's so nosey. I love her.

"I want to try!" Honey declares.

"Want to try? On whom?" I ask.

"You! Show me what he did."

My Stars move around the bed excitedly. It's not anything they probably haven't done with each other. They are always trying new toys—straps, devices, plugs, and more. I mean Lucy has a whole room of toys.

"Fine. Come here, Honey." Her lips part and her pupils expand. She's so excited.

When we all mess around in bed together, I usually excuse myself. This will be the first time since the Pack House that we all take part. Carmen and Lucy each pull my thong down and then part my legs. I'm wearing a satin teddy, and they pull down the straps, revealing my breasts.

Honey sits between my legs on her knees.

"I want to see you come. While I'm happy to hear that some random man got you there, your pack deserves your pleasure, don't you think?"

Honey purrs when she talks. She makes the most money out of any of us at the club. She's the most beautiful woman. She's exceptionally tall, and her curves can get men to go to war for her. It's hard not to look at her with lust. She's a walking dream.

"Yes, ma'am."

Carmen and Lucy settle on either side of me, then start licking my neck. Tara cleans the toy and then brings it to Honey. She thanks her with a kiss on the lips.

God. They are so beautiful.

Forming our pack was the most natural thing. We'd all been hired to work at the O'Bannon Pack House at different times. There were other girls there too, but our friendship was like magic. We understood each other. We didn't like being apart. Pretty soon we started bunking at Carmen's apartment until we were living on top of each other there.

Packs always carry the last name of the alpha with the most influence, a special alpha power. Since we have no alphas, we chose a new name—Pack Star. Named for the five points. Five Stars.

They are my stars.

Each of us has star tattoos.

Carmen moves down my neck and sucks my nipple into her mouth. My back bows and my head falls back.

"Oh god. Oh god. That feels so good! Fuck me!"

Lucy takes my other breast into her mouth. Sucking and teasing with her teeth and tongue. It sends my pussy to flight. It's so fucking good. Honey holds my hip down, so it stops humping the air, and then turns on the vibrator.

"I hope this alpha didn't try to steal you from us, Sauv. You're ours. You are ours to kiss, suck, fuck, and love—do you hear me?"

"Yes!" I cry out. Having my tits teased and sucked like this is sending me to another fucking plane.

Tara comes up next to Lucy and curls around to kiss me.

"We think you're so fuckin hot. So, hot. Your ass is a goddamned marvel," she says over my lips and then draws my tongue in her mouth. I chase her kiss until we are lewdly making out.

Honey rests the stick on my pussy, waiting for my body to open up to her.

"Oh baby," she moans into my thigh. "Oh my god, Sauv."

"I could suck on these titties forever," Carmen groans. Lucy agrees but doesn't stop flicking my nipple with her strong tongue.

Honey brings the vibrations to my clit and then enters me with two of her fingers. Pretty quickly she starts fuckin me with her fingers, and pressing the toy into my clit.

"I'm going to fuckin come!" I scream.

"Good, my darling. Come for your girlfriends. We want to take you over the edge."

Honey's fingers are relentless. Carmen and Lucy are working my tits. And Tara kisses me like she's in love with me.

The best part is I love her too.

I come.

"Oh my god!" I scream. Everyone's mouths turn soft and they lick me tenderly and kiss me sweetly as my body spasms. Carmen doesn't waste time. She flips me over onto my shaky knees, then lays down, directing me to straddle her face. I hold onto the headboard, trying to make sense of the horizon line. I turn to look over my shoulder, and Honey lays on her stomach between Carmen's legs and is already eating her out.

"Oh god, Honey, you are way too fucking good at that!" Carmen says, and then pulls my hips down over her face. This is a little advanced for me. I've seen the other girls face sit. Hell, I've seen them face sit other people, too, but I didn't do this kind of thing with Legs.

Carmen licks up my wet folds, then latches her whole mouth onto my clit, working her jaw. All thoughts of my dead ex-boyfriend fly out the window.

"Fuuuuck!" I hit my head into the wall, but don't even feel a thing.

Lucy comes over and kisses my neck and also puts her hand on the wall for my head to hit up against. Lucy loves me.

"I love watching you come," she says in my ear. "I've been dying to hear you cry out in real pleasure, my love."

Lucy loves me, and I love her.

I come, quickly and without stopping, all over Carmen's mouth. My legs give out and Lucy catches me. She pulls me off Carmen, and brings me into her arms.

Carmen comes next, and then I hear Honey and Tara come on each other's fingers. The chorus of our panting and cries of pleasure reverberates through me, and Lucy holds me tight as my body trembles. The other girls also pull in closer, throwing arms and legs over me. Their love for me seeps into my bones. Tears prick at the edges of my eyes. I keep thinking about what I wouldn't do for them.

"She's crashing," Lucy tells everyone. Sure enough, I'm shaking like a leaf and crying. They hold me and tell me everything they love about me. They tell me they will always love me.

My heart feels cracked up and I feel incredibly exposed. Life seems so tragically weak, and yet incredibly overwhelming.

I let them cocoon me in their affection until I'm able to normalize. Or stabilize.

Each girl, exhausted and satiated, falls asleep in our pile. When I open my eyes, feeling a lot more normal, I see Carmen is still awake.

"Carmen?" I ask.

"Yes, my love."

"I hope you know, I would do it again. Everything, as long as it would lead me here to all of you again."

"Sauvignon, I look up to you so much. I know everyone views me as the leader, but I'd be nowhere without you. You've sacrificed so much for us. Don't think I don't know what you did for us. You are the real leader. The center of our star. The core."

There's so many things I want to tell her. I want to tell her how she's saved me so many times. How she's my rock, and I want to tell her I would follow her anywhere. But she wants me to get better, and for the first time in a long time, I do too.

The core of their star shouldn't be dying.

"I think I need to see a therapist."

She smiles warmly at me.

"What a great idea."

With my star holding me together, I finally drift off to sleep.

Chapter 7

Monroe

Sepp finally walks through the door at an ungodly hour. I can't remember if he's ever been missing before. I'm huddled in my nest in the back corner, buried in my blankets, and crying.

Omegas cry all the time, so it's not weird for me.

And I'm not crying over those loser alphas.

I'm not crying over anything actually.

Really.

I pull the blanket over my head making sure my face is exposed so when my terrible alpha comes in, I can see his stupid face.

I'm so incredibly angry at Sepp!

He must be dumb or an asshole, but I can't figure out which it is. My inner omega wanted him and only him for my heat, and when he finally caved and fucked me, I wanted for nothing. I've never felt anything like that. His big, mammoth body curled over me, delicately touching my back like he worshipped me. Oh my god, I could come just thinking about it. And then he left! He fucking left my nest that I begged him to join me in!

He rejected me!

Then he had the audacity to try to apologize to me for the whole thing. Which only made me realize he regretted our time together. Anyone would be hurt! I wanted to hurt him back, so I threw my toast at his dumb, beautiful head, but toast doesn't do anything. It was a stupid try. Sepp is a foot taller than me and has hands like bear paws. I could never actually hurt him.

He knocks gently at the door of my nest.

"Come in!" You big dumb, dummy.

Sepp enters with a shopping bag. He gets down on his knees and crawls to me. He's so good with omegas. He knows he's a huge alpha, and approaching me with his full height might be seen as intimidating, so he lowers himself. He gets close, looking at my face peaking out through the comforter, and smiles.

He's glowing.

The alpha is glowing!

My lips part in surprise.

"Omega Monroe, I got some things for you. If you don't like any of these things, we can go back."

I narrow my eyes at him.

"Why do you seem so...refreshed?"

He always thinks through things for a long time before reacting. He is taking a lot of time to process my question, and when he does, his face gets all red.

He's blushing.

"What happened?!"

Oh no...did someone steal my alpha? Instantly, big fat tears roll down my face. Sepp shuffles closer, and I pull the blanket over my face.

"No, no, no...Monroe. Wait, come back out. Let me explain."

"You're an asshole!" I regret it immediately. Sepp is my handler. We aren't in a real relationship. He's supposed to care for me until I find a pack. If he found someone, he may leave me for them!

"No, baby, it's not like that. Come on out." He picks at the blankets, trying to extract me from them.

Did he just call me baby? I relax and let him pull the blanket enough to poke his head inside with me.

His apricot smell surrounds me, calming me.

"Tell me? Tell me what you want more than anything?"

Another charming line.

I take a deep inhale of his scent, drowning in it. I want to taste his cock, have his scent pushed down into my throat. Coat my insides with it.

"I don't know."

"Tell me, do you love beta women?"

It's then that I smell the beta on him. A female beta.

"What?"

"There's a pack of beta women, five of them, that are looking for an omega."

My forehead creases even more, then I bare my omega teeth at him, a sign of disrespect.

"And you fucked them?"

His hand finds my thigh in the mess of blankets, and he rests it there.

"One of them, Sauvignon. I want you to meet her pack."

The omega in me lifts his head in interest. Did Sepp...get a pack for me?

"What're you saying?"

"There's a pack of five beta women looking for an omega. I met one—Sauvignon. She's beautiful. She made my heart stop. Will you come with me to meet them?"

I don't want to get too excited. Sepp really is saying he vetted a pack for me. He does everything else for me, why am I so surprised? Maybe I'm surprised that he knows me so well. The idea of five beta women makes my dick hard. It sends my heart into flight.

I follow a beta woman's Patronage online and am first to watch every new video she posts. She's a femme Domme who posts spicy scenes between her and a cute blonde woman who acts out BDSM scenes. They don't show their faces. I'm too scared to even comment or message, all I do is watch...

Sepp smiles at my reaction.

"Right now?"

"No, this Thursday. They work at Flash House. We will see them dance, and you can tell me what you think..."

"They're... strippers?"

My cock leaks. I grab it, pushing it down.

"Yes. And more."

"Sepp! I can't go to a strip club!"

"Why not?"

"I'll have a heart attack!"

He chuckles flippantly at me, and his hand squeezes my thigh. While I'm no newbie when it comes to sex, I've only been with male alphas. Sepp knows that I have a thing for beta girls, but he's also aware that I've never even gotten close to them. They make me nervous! Maybe it's because I like them so much that I'm afraid to talk to them.

"You'll be fine. I'll be there."

In another intimate move, Sepp kisses me on my nose and then retreats from my blanket fort.

"I'm going to bed, do you need anything?"

Rendered completely speechless, I just shake my head no.

"Ok, goodnight, omega."

He shuts the door and I groan, then bury myself further into the blankets. What the hell just happened?

Thursday comes so quickly and I didn't, not once, figure out how to prepare myself. I did stalk their social media and found who I think are the beta pack. I know about Sauvignon, obviously. Though I couldn't find any videos of her dancing. There's Honey. She's this curvy Latina that would break me in two, and I'd ask her to do it again. Tara, a sweet looking blonde who dances to bubblegum pop music and wears pink. Lucy, a dominatrix type...

Carmen, definitely. She's got red hair, tattoos all down her legs, and is the best dancer that I could see.

It makes my head hurt.

These women are beautiful. They could have the world. Why would they ever want a soft-spoken omega with an average sized cock who will probably be incapable of even speaking to them?

If they touch me, I'll pass out.

I come out of my bathroom wearing a black t-shirt and my nice black jeans. I have my favorite Jordan's in my hands, making sure the laces are tidy, when I stop short. Sepp stands in the living room, tapping on his phone, looking like a fucking wet dream. He's wearing a blue velvet sports coat over a silk black button up, and perfectly tailored slacks. His hair is styled back, and his hands are covered in gold and silver rings. Pack Foxx probably gave him some of these rings, but I swear I've never seen him this done up.

"I'm not going," I declare and turn around.

Sepp pockets his phone and races after me grabbing my shoulder and turning me around. I can't meet his eyes, so I close mine.

"Monroe! Don't be silly. Look at me."

I shake my head.

"Why don't you want to go?"

I can't tell him it's because he looks too good.

Never mind, I'm an omega. I can say whatever I want.

"You will steal them all from me."

"What?"

"You look way too good, Sepp. You look like you own the place."

He chuckles and pushes my chin up.

"You look good, too."

"Call me baby."

"What?"

"I liked when you called me baby the other day. Call me baby and I'll come."

He is quiet for a long time, so I finally open up my eyes.

His beautiful, sweet face is so close to mine.

"Come on, baby, let's go."

My entire body shivers.

I love when he denies me nothing.

I follow him out to a car he ordered. We both want to drink tonight so we need someone else to drive. Sepp opens the door for me and I slip inside.

It's not too far, about 30 minutes away.

I'm so full of nervous energy I could pop. We pull up to the club around 10 o'clock at night. There are lights everywhere. The line of cars dropping off patrons is so damned long. I sigh and bounce my leg, waiting for our turn. Girls in beautiful tight dresses greet people exiting the cars.

"This is a nice club for a topless bar," Sepp says.

"What do you mean?"

"Usually the topless bars are kind of skanky. This one is nice. I heard the dancers are really talented. Someone said they are like professional athletes, and train all week."

Well, that's all the info I need. I open the car door and take off my seat belt at the same time. Sepp jumps over me and pulls the door back closed.

"Get off me! I'm going to go run into traffic!"

"I know! I'm stopping you!"

I try to push the door and he just holds it closed.

We move up in the line.

There's not really traffic out there. If I got out, I'd just be on the sidewalk, but he knows what I mean.

"Here, take my hand. Anytime you feel the need to jump out into traffic, just hold my hand."

Sepp interlaces our fingers.

His hand dwarfs mine.

I take a deep breath, and his apricot scent calms me.

"Fine."

Though his hand in mine might not be enough. I may need his hand on a different part of me. Would he do that with me? The hurt feeling of how he left me during my heat comes back. He can't just call me baby, kiss my nose, and hold my hand and then tell me later how much he regrets it. I'll die.

"I want an apology," I say suddenly.

"For what?" Call me baby...

"For how rude you've been to me since my heat."

"What?"

We move up to another place in line.

"I begged for you to join me and then after you knotted me I woke up to find you gone, and then you told me how much you wish you hadn't been with me. You hurt my feelings, Sepp."

He turns away, thinking. I always have to remember to give Sepp plenty of time to think.

"I'm sorry," he says. "I didn't think you were in your right mind to consent to us being together. I took advantage of your state..."

"That's stupid. I feel like I made myself clear."

"Oh, shit," the rideshare driver says over his music, "Sorry, we were in the wrong line. This is valet. I have to circle the block and get in the right line."

"That's fine, we aren't in a rush. I'll make sure to tip you."

"Appreciate it," he says, then turns his music back up on his front speakers.

Sepp turns to me, and says, "I don't regret it. It was the best thing that happened to me."

My breath quickens. He's going to say something awful isn't he? He's going to say it was the best thing that happened to him, and then tell me how he will never be part of my heat ever, ever, ever, ever again.

Sepp grabs my face.

"I'm sorry. I didn't want to upset you. I was being honest..."

"It was the best thing that happened to me, too."

He smiles, and I let his beauty shine around me. His delicious apricot smell, and my coconut smell mingle.

"Are you excited to meet the pack?"

The subject change ramps my heart rate up again.

"Sepp, what if they don't like me? Most beta women aren't looking for a man like me."

His eyebrows wrinkle.

"What do you mean?"

"Like, I'm not like a male beta or male alpha, I'm different."

My hands are sweaty and my breath keeps coming in quickly.

Sepp turns and grabs me by my waist, pulling me off the seat and into his body. He hugs me close and rubs my back. I settle into him.

"Omega," he purrs, and I press into his warmth, seeking his own heartbeat to regulate mine. "No one can resist an omega, especially not you."

His hand strokes down until it reaches my belt, and he hesitates.

"Everything about you is attractive. Your eyes. Your voice. Your body."

To punctuate his point, his hand slides down over my ass, not my cheek, but my crack. His strong fingers rub between my ass, gliding over my jean covered asshole. The sensation is wild. It sends lightning up and down my bones. I bow into him. He does it again.

"Baby," he whispers, and I'm fucking done for. My dick is trapped in my jeans, and I press it into his body, rubbing over him, as he continues to rake his fingers over my ass.

"More," I moan, and he speeds up, stroking me up and down. I nuzzle into his neck and hold on to the front of his shirt. "Sepp. More. Please."

He grunts in my ear, and now I'm nearly done for.

"I want you nice and relaxed before we go in there," he murmurs.

"Then don't stop, please."

I reach down and quickly undo my belt and jeans, pulling my cock out. Sepp doesn't stop rubbing my ass, but with his free hand, he reaches between us and takes my cock, then gives me a tight, delicious squeeze.

"More," I whine.

It's not lost on me that the driver is a mere arm's length away. But he's a beta, so he may not know what we are up to, or maybe I really don't care. I look out the tinted window and see we are nearly to the front.

"Please," I beg. "Please, alpha."

Sepp pumps my cock and stimulates my ass, and without warning, I come. I come from both places at once and it feels like I've exploded.

Which I have, all over his hand.

My body is limp and relaxed. My heart is full. Wow! Sepp is incredible. No one has ever made me feel like that. It was just what I needed.

He puts my cock back into my pants and does my belt, setting me in my seat.

"We've arrived."

I look up at the rear-view mirror to see some knowing, smirking eyes staring back at me.

Sepp turns my face to his and kisses me right on the lips.

If this were an animation, I'd have little bubble hearts popping around my head. Sepp brings me to strip clubs to make my dreams come true. He's the best alpha.

"You feel better?"

"Yes, alpha. Thank you."

Chapter 8

Monroe

S epp pulls us both out of the car and in front of the club. Two big spotlights flank the front doors. The crowd is ravenous.

I decide right then and there to let go of my fears. I may be shy when it comes to beta women, and I may be self conscious of my omega body, but I can't let that hold me back.

Not tonight.

Sepp's hand wrung that fear out of my cock. If he thinks I'll like these women, then he must be right. I may only know about sex through fucking alphas, but who cares! I'm holding Sepp's hand. We are going to do this together.

Plus, it's just a meeting.

Sepp leans down, and says, "You have nothing to be nervous about. Everyone in there is going to either want to be you, or fuck you."

My skin prickles.

"Have some courage."

"Yes. Courage," I repeat. Then I take a deep breath and nod. I can't help but agree when he's this close, when we did what we just did in the car. Sepp will always take care of me. He's my courage.

He interlaces our fingers, which surprises the hell out of me, and we walk into the club. It's dark and loud, even in this front room. I can smell everything. From the alphas throwing their pheromones around, the sweat and alcohol from all the mixed drinks, and that fake fog machine smell.

I love beta girls for so many reasons, like their subtle scents. It absolutely thrills me. They smell like women and it is euphoric.

I doubt I can get that scent in a place like this.

I'm free to get in because I'm an omega—always a delight to be given free stuff—but Sepp pays his door fee. The gorgeous beta woman takes his money and checks him out with a heated look. I give my best back-the-hell-off glare. And she does. She backs off. Probably because we are holding hands.

What a sight we must be? Alpha and omega, holding hands, about to enter a strip club. I wish I could see us together like this. I bet I'd be a little jealous. Sepp is so handsome, and he's got me, the precious male omega.

"Is Sauvignon working tonight?" he asks the woman at the counter.

"Oh Alpha, you're just going to have to go in there and see which talent we have tonight. I promise, you won't be disappointed."

He frowns.

His weight shifts.

Is Sepp nervous? That would be ironic. It's usually me who's nervous.

I pull on his hand.

"Come on. You dragged me all the way here, the least we can do is enter the damned club."

Sepp gives me a small smile. I nod to the curtained doorway, ripe with the unknown.

"I'm sure she's here. She said she would be here, right?"

"You're right. Let's go."

He takes the first step in Flash House. Pushing through the big curtain, there's a long, tight hallway that leads downwards. The hallways gets smaller as it descends, so Sepp has to duck down. The further we get, the louder the music is. At the bottom, it's like we've arrived in another plane of existence. The hallway opens up to the large club.

The real world feels so far away.

"Wow, this is incredible!" I say. A platform runs from one side of the club and splits into two other parts, forming a river-like shape leading off into parts unknown. Large chandeliers hang heavy from the ceiling and poles dot the stage. There are half a dozen bars, all managed by gorgeous girls. I can't believe the amount of hidden space, raised lounges, dance floors, and observation decks.

As someone who experiences a lot of social anxiety, a place like this would normally send me for the hills, but I spot at least three safe zones.

I lead Sepp to one of them. Two seats that are right next to the stage, but in the far left part of the building, near a bar with only one bartender. It's hidden but safe.

Sepp and I sit down and look out at the empty stage. Obviously the girls won't come dance over here unless they see a patron, so for now, girls dance in the main room of Flash House, and we wait. A blonde girl in a lace skirt that only covers an inch of her hips and nothing else, including her entire thong clad ass, saunters over to us. She's wearing a little lace visor too, giving off the perfect cigarette girl look. Her face brightens as she gets closer.

"She's so cute..." I whisper to myself. Wow! She's as short as I am, and everything about her is cute and round. I could play with her for days.

Her bubblegum pink lips say something to me, and all I hear is the whooshing of blood in my own ears.

I've never seen a girl like this before. It makes me wonder if this is even real life. She puts her hand on my chair and leans down to repeat herself, her breasts in my face. She's wearing a little lace top and most of her is spilling from both the top and bottom.

Again, I can't hear anything.

I do see her mouth move, forming the word "omega."

That's it. I'm done for.

You could say male omegas are strange. Very rare and often shorter than most men, we have feminine features, and our cocks aren't big like an alpha's. We don't behave like male betas or alphas, with aggression or chauvinism. We require care and adoration.

Would she prefer someone like Sepp, though he is not your average alpha. He may be big and tall, but he's sweet and thoughtful. He didn't fuck me hard either—he was careful. He may have just been careful with me, though, because he knows how I like it.

It makes me nervous to think maybe I'm not her type.

I guess there's only one way to know...

"Monroe," Sepp says to me. I turn and look at him. "She's asking what you want to drink."

I turn back and see her beam at me. She's like the sun. She has to be glowing. It's blinding me.

"Oh, sorry, I'll have a vodka cranberry."

She turns to Sepp.

"I'll have the same."

Her fingers touch my wrist. "Coming right up, baby."

Baby.

My body shivers, and I try to stand up, to do what, I don't know. Sepp puts his hand on my thigh and pushes me back down.

"I think that was one of them. Tara!" I say and he looks past me to see her leaning over the bar to tell them our order. Her ass is all the way out of her skirt.

"I think you're right."

Sepp didn't get Sauvignon's number, so they haven't been in contact since they met at the sex toy shop. He's almost just as blind as me.

Pretty soon the hottest woman I've ever seen in my entire life dances down the platform toward us. She stops at some of the poles dotting the platform to twirl, so we see her whole, practically naked body. Most of the girls have fishnets or armbands, skirts, and cute layered tops. But this woman looks naked. When she turns, I see little red hearts covering her nipples, held up by thin red strings.

"Please welcome to the stage, your next potential girlfriend—Honey Star!" the DJ announces her over the speakers. I'm surprised, and also not, that she isn't using a stage name. Or maybe Honey is her stage name?

A sexy, heavy bass song blasts around the club.

Honey is actually wearing a thong that I didn't even notice was there on her warm brown skin until she's closer. She quickly disposes of a tiny bra and shows off her stunning breasts to the two of us. My eyes lose focus, and all I see is the most shapely woman swaying her ass, getting lower and lower to the floor. More people rush to take up seats around this side of the platform. The place is getting more and more crowded.

I focus only on Honey—a smoke show of a woman. She could have any man or woman she wants I bet. Her skin glitters and her pink wig flows as she swings around the pole, then throws her legs in the air. Her thighs jiggle in a way that instantly makes me hard.

Her eyes go right to me as she hangs upside down and then clacks her pleaser shoes together. The sound makes me jump.

Drool gathers at my mouth. The lights flash and suddenly she's crawling towards me, her breasts swinging. They are the perfect shape. God did something amazing when he made her.

She leans over the edge of the stage, grabs my chair and pulls me close, putting her face in my neck and breathing me in.

"Oh my god!" I shout, and as she retreats, she kisses my cheek. I look at Sepp, horrified and aroused.

He smiles encouragingly at me.

Do they do this with everyone, or do they know who I am?

As I watch Honey shake her ass, showing her barely covered pussy just inches from my face, Sepp seems to read my mind. He leans in and says, "I don't think they know anything except that you're an omega. I think she thinks you're cute."

That's insane!

I take some cash from Sepp's large stack and set a few dollars on the stage. Honey thanks me, leaving the money, and does some insanely erotic moves on the pole. I clap as she descends, catching herself.

Sepp tosses some money as well. I take some more, but before I can toss it, Honey offers me her hip to put it in her string. I stand and lean over the stage, and with shaking hands, in a move I didn't even know I was capable of, I slide the money into her panty string. She rewards me with another kiss on my cheek, and then rubs her bare breasts over my face.

I didn't know there would be so much touching!

I crash into my seat in a daze. She finishes her routine, and another woman, nearly as tall, in a full body green lace bodysuit, helps her gather her tips. The announcer says the next dancer's name: Carmen.

She has a high pony of red hair and swings it around, then slaps into the pole. She grabs the pole with one hand and then slowly drops down, showing off the cut out heart at the top of her ass in her bodysuit.

Over her shoulder, her eyes hit mine. She has smoky eyes, and based on looks alone, she could tell me to do anything, and I'd do it.

She could eat me up...

I yelp and squirm in my seat.

Sepp throws money immediately. Good job, Sepp, I think she may kick us out if we don't.

Her routine is insane. She has impeccable control. I throw some cash, and she crooks her finger at me. She wants me to get closer.

I obey, like a good boy, standing up and moving to the stage. It comes up to just below my hips. She sits down on the stage and wraps both legs around me, then moves with the music, up and down, imitating fucking me. I'm standing, and she's still on the stage. She takes my hand and pets herself down the middle, my thumb grazes her nipple on her very large breasts that are trapped under green lace, and then goes over her belly button piercing.

She can have the rest of the money!

I'm going to be so broke.

She grinds against my hard dick and smiles at me like we share a secret. Then she grabs my face and licks me up the side. The crowd goes wild.

To me, an omega, it feels like a claim.

My inner omega decides we are hers from now until death. She's claimed me, and I accept.

"Wow," is all I manage to say. Her approving smile is all I want.

"What's your name, handsome?"

"Monroe," I offer like it's all I have.

She smiles and then works her entire body over mine. Her heat and energy are something I'll remember forever.

She moves away, working on her routine, and my eyeballs are now just hearts shooting out of my eyes.

The man next to me laughs, and when I turn to look at him, he says, "Don't let that get to your head, kid. She's a stripper trying to get tips, is all."

All the levity and excitement deflates from me in an instant.

"She got you good!" He laughs again, and I look at my shoes.

She did get me good.

I turn to Sepp who is looking at her like she's a marvel, then I finally look at the crowd. So many hungry faces, half in love with her. She finishes her routine and leaves.

"Hey," Sepp says with a huge smile. Another girl, not someone from Pack Star, is dancing now. "Let's go get another drink!"

I nod my head, looking down at my empty one. He takes my hand, and we head over to the bar just as someone is walking in from the back.

Sepp stops short at seeing the bartender. She's a stunning Black woman with beautiful bouncy hair and a shiny gold nose ring. She has gold dust swirling all over her skin, and is wearing a gold bra and cheetah print mini skirt.

Sauvignon.

Sepp is catatonic.

He's in love.

There's no other explanation.

Sauvignon looks up and sees him, mirroring that "deer in head-lights" look he has on his face.

It's hitting me how real this all is.

He's fallen head over heels for this woman. With the flashing lights, loud music, confusing smells, and now my heart being torn up from all the competing emotions, like how much I'm enamoured with the

Star girls, I decide now is the time to tell Sepp what I've wanted to tell him before my heat.

I tug his hand, and he looks at me to see what I want.

"I'm in love with you, Sepp!" I shout, then I leave my mouth open to say more, but I'm unable to find more words. I can't believe I just said that!

Out loud!

Sepp told me to be courageous and I just followed that right over the edge, didn't I? Oh my god.

His reaction is late.

Sepp is always so careful with me, so he isn't saying anything back right away. I know he's just taking his time to think, but every second he takes worries me.

The worry turns into anger.

Why isn't he saying anything back!

Sepp opens his mouth and shuts it.

That's it. I can't do this. I'm much too sensitive.

I run.

I run down a corridor to the bathrooms, but take a random door that turns out to be a private dance room. It's small as hell. Maybe five feet by five feet. That's fine.

I can cry in here.

Sepp is pissing me off! First with fucking me and then telling me he regretted it. Then rubbing my ass and cock until I came in his hand! Now taking his sweet time to tell me he loves me back.

I understand he's my handler, and that comes with ramifications. I know this. I know that he could get removed from the clan if they think he's taking advantage of me. At least that's what any clan would do! But we don't know that!

He asked me to be courageous, but where's his courage!?

Suddenly, two women rush into the room with me. One of them pushes the other into the door, and they start making out.

They don't see or notice me.

I make myself as small and quiet as possible so they don't get startled. There's an armchair that I squeeze behind, braced against the wall. I recognize them almost immediately. Honey and Carmen. The dancers. Honey rips down Carmen's green bodysuit, then thrusts her fingers in Carmen's wet cunt. I can smell and hear how wet she is. My cock is immediately hard.

"There's a male omega out there!" Honey says over Carmen's lips as she fucks her with her fingers. "He's so cute, did you see him?"

Cute?

"The guy with the cool black hair? He's got princess eyes."

I hold my teeth shut until they ache, preventing myself from making any of my omega noises. This room is not that big! My heart pumps wildly. I shouldn't be listening to this...

"Didn't Sauv say that the alpha she hooked up with was going to bring his omega by?" Carmen says with a quivering voice, closer and closer to climaxing.

"Oh my god is that him?" Honey licks Carmen's breast then sucks one of her nipples. Her breasts are so much more amazing than they were on stage, covered by the see-through green lace.

I need to speak up, but my ears do that whooshing thing, and my vision tunnels to just her breasts.

This is the most erotic thing I've ever witnessed. Being trapped in here is both my dream, and nightmare.

"I had my ass in his face. Maybe I should have been more gentle with the lamb."

I make eye contact with Carmen, and she gasps, but I think half that gasp was from what Honey is doing to her body.

"Oh Car, your cunt is especially wet tonight," Honey moans.

"It's that..." she keeps her eyes right on mine as she says, "It's that the omega. He's just so pretty."

"Are you thinking about him while I've got my fingers in you?"

"Yes!"

Honey uses more of her fingers and goes back to sucking her breast.

Carmen isn't going to tell Honey that I'm here. Oh my god! She challenges me with her eyes on if I will say anything either. Honey is flicking it with her beautiful long acrylic nails, and I no longer have control over my tongue.

But shouldn't she tell Honey they have company? Why do I have to do it! She knows, too!

Instead, she keeps her eyes on me while she reaches down and also strokes her packmate's cunt.

"Yes, Carmen, please. Let's come together." Honey lifts her leg over Carmen's hip and humps her against the door, slamming into her over and over again. Her ass shakes in a way that makes my whole body so warm I'm going to catch on fire.

She's so sexy. They both are. I can't fucking breathe.

"I wonder if he can handle all of us."

"He'd never get a break. We'd all want to fuck him 24/7."

Oh my god.

"Every morning sucking him dry. Every afternoon hand jobs from five sets of hands. And then riding him repeatedly all night."

And with that—I come in my pants.

I didn't even fucking touch myself. I grab on to my mouth, and my cock spills into my jeans.

Carmen follows shortly after me. She's coming just from looking at me. Honey comes too, and they pant and hold each other. Carmen whispers in Honey's ear, and her body jolts in surprise.

She told her I'm here.

"Hello..." Carmen says with her dark, sultry voice as she holds Honey, who is smiling ear to ear.

<h1 style="text-align:center">Chapter 9</h1>

Monroe

"I'm Carmen and this is Honey, my pack mate. What's your name, handsome?"

I debate lying. Or running. But they are blocking the door. I should just tell them the truth.

"I'm Monroe. Sorry, I didn't mean to watch you two. I just needed a place to hide..."

"Oh, sweet omega," Honey says and turns around. My entire body shakes. I think I'm afraid. I'm afraid she'll call me a pervert or a weirdo. I'm afraid she'll reject me. "Did you get the nesties?"

I huff out a small laugh.

Omegas nest in small little spaces. It brings them comfort.

I don't know what else to say. She's so beautiful. And now both of their scents are saturating this room, so I can't think straight. Honey smells like honey. Unironically. Carmen smells like hot cocoa. Betas don't usually have scent profiles, but as an omega, I'm sensitive to these things.

Plus, I'm looking out for it.

"Um..." nothing else comes out.

I look away.

"No, we are sorry. We didn't see you there."

"It's ok."

They wait to see if I do anything. I'm waiting for them to leave. Not that I want them to. But I just don't know what else could possibly happen.

"Since we are here, did you want a private dance?" Honey offers in a calm voice, like she's afraid she'll spook me.

"No, it's ok."

"You don't want us?" Her words cut through me. I peek at the girls. Their clothes are barely on. Carmen's tits are out showing off her stunning light brown nipples. My pants are still sticky from earlier. If they saw...

"You're Sepp's omega, right? The one that Sauvignon met the other day?"

I manage a nod.

I'm not exactly his omega, but I like the way it sounds. I also like that they know who I am.

"Should we go get him?"

"No."

Honey and Carmen exchange a look.

I creep out from behind the armchair, still staying close to the wall. I don't want them to leave. I want to do what they did together, but with me, too.

I have to have courage.

"I'm just a little shy...around girls. I think you're so beautiful and it makes it hard to think straight, or to know what to say."

Honey smiles warmly at me.

"You should sit down, Monroe," Carmen says. She's my beta. I've already agreed to do anything she says, so I do as I'm told and walk in front of the chair, nearly touching the woman, and then sit down.

"Would you like a private dance?"

"Yes, ma'am." I pull out the folded cash from my pocket.

"Oh my god, you're so prepared," they coo.

I was worried about the money part of this. How it works. How it would make me feel. But having something I can give them in return makes me feel a little less anxious.

"Do you have anything off limits, Monroe? Because I don't. Anything is on the table," Honey purrs, bending down, letting her tits come close to my face. She's wearing her top, a string bikini top with little red nipple covers in the shape of hearts. Possessed by my own intense desires, I lift my hand up and run my finger along the top of the heart. Her brown nipples peak out over the sides. Round shapes are hard to cover with heart shapes.

She makes a pretty sound.

I drop my hand and look into her eyes.

"Limits? I don't think so," I answer, my voice still a little low. "But, I'm kind of..."

"What?"

"I've only been with alphas. Male alphas."

"Don't tell us that, it'll make us feel special."

"You are special. To me."

I think my words melted the two Stars.

Carmen shakes her head, waking herself up, then comes around me, placing her hands on my shoulders and leaning over the back of the chair, and whispers, "Can we touch you?"

"Yes."

She slides her hands down my chest and burrows her face in my neck, licking me fervently.

I jump in my seat.

Honey drops to her knees, parting my legs wider. Her hands rest on my inner thighs.

"Anywhere you don't want to be touched?"

"Touch me wherever you want, beta. I'm yours."

I've decided I belong to Honey, too.

My words please her. Her eyes roll back with her head, giving me a beautiful view of her long pretty neck, and she caresses my leg until she feels the wet spot from when I came in my pants. Her head pops back up, and she gives me a devious look as her thumb strokes the spot.

I'm unable to look away as she brings her thumb to her mouth and sucks.

"How does it taste?" I ask, the desperation in my voice undeniable. I need her to like it.

"Yum."

Fuck yes.

Carmen nips at my skin, and I jump again.

"How do you feel about pain?"

"Pain? Like spanking?"

"Yes!" Honey says. "We should punish Carmen for not telling me there was a hidden omega in this room while we messed around. That was a mean thing she pulled."

"Punish?" I ask, confused.

"Honey, you have the best ideas, my love. You will spank me for my crimes."

Carmen comes around to the side of the chair and crawls across my lap, laying on the arms of the chair. Her ass is right in my lap. She turns over her shoulder to look at me when she feels my dick get hard; she moans.

It just makes me get harder. I like this, but goddamned my brain is on fire. I don't know where to focus, or what to think, or even what to do!

"How many does she deserve, Monroe?"

I set my hand down on her thigh and then pull it away, realizing it's all skin. Carmen is no longer wearing her lace bodysuit, but now just a thong going right between her perfectly plump cheeks.

"One?"

"But she was so naughty!"

Honey's hand strokes one of Carmen's cheeks, charming me with the motion, and then she pulls back and slaps. Her ass jiggles and she squirms. I quickly place my hand where she slapped.

"Oh my god!" I say, mostly alarmed. I see the red mark over her skin and she squirms underneath me.

I've seen spanking videos online, I've just never had someone in my lap like this. I've never done it before. My old alphas would just fuck my ass and suck me off. I'd suck them off too. We were always just trying to get to that climax. No finesse.

You can watch every BDSM video from your favorite femme domme, but until you have a beautiful woman in your lap begging to be spanked, you'll never truly know. I rub the spot.

"One more?" I ask.

"Yes, I think at least one more."

Honey slaps her again, and we both moan. I rub the spot, wanting to feel her raw skin.

"Again."

Honey slaps her again, and it is like its own small climax, but without the fall.

"How are you feeling, Carmen?" Honey checks in with her, turning her face so she can see.

"Monroe is so hard underneath me," she says.

How can I help it!

"Maybe Monroe needs a turn punishing you."

"Honey, you always have the best ideas. Do you want to spank me, Monroe? I mean, I didn't tell Honey that you were in the room. I was staring right at you when she made me come all over her pretty fingers."

I hold my hand up and slap her ass, making my palm skip over the skin. She moans even louder and I can smell how turned on that made her. So, I do it again.

And again.

Three is enough.

Nevermind, one more.

I slap her again, and she curls around me.

"Oh my god, Monroe. You're good at that."

Those femme domme videos taught me something, afterall. Maybe I'm not so inexperienced.

Honey and I help Carmen off of me, and she chooses to sit at my feet next to her pack mate, and push me back into the chair.

"Was that good, Carmen?"

"Oh, yes Sweet Thing. That was good. My ass is very sore."

They look so beautiful looking up at me, and I feel almost high. Is this what doing kinky stuff does to someone?

"Monroe."

"Yes?"

Carmen lets the silence come in. I take a few full breaths as I wait for her to say something.

"Are you shy?"

"Yes."

She smiles at my sincerity.

"Where do you work, Sweet Thing?"

"Work?"

"Yeah, what do you do?"

I relax completely at her questions.

"I'm in school."

"What do you study?"

"Painting."

Both girls smile. They like that I said that.

"My clan thinks I should go to a big art school, but the community college has a great program. I'm learning a lot."

"That's awesome. Where do you live?"

I perk up.

"Near the college! With Sepp. We have a nice apartment nearby, and I can walk, but he always drives me."

"Honey thinks we should go to cosmetology school."

"Oh! You should. My college is a technical school, and they have an entire program. I always see so many beta girls walking to class..."

"We could go to school together!" Honey says.

My cheeks get so hot I have to put my hands on them to cool them down.

"You're the sweetest thing," Carmen says with a sigh.

"Do you really think so?"

I drop my hands from my cheeks, and then set one on Honey's hand and the other on Carmen's.

"I don't give compliments unless I mean them, and you are sweet, and so very handsome."

I stroke their hands, feeling their soft skin.

"Our pack is looking for an omega. Did you know that?"

"Yes. Sepp told me. That's why we're here."

"Are you open to being courted?" Carmen asks.

I can't imagine she said that right? She's bold! But she's got me feeling so good with everything they've done today. I feel like the world is spinning around us and only us.

"I..." I can't tell her that I already feel like hers. Omega ways can scare regular people, but Carmen is being attentive. She doesn't look scared.

"I want that. I want to get to know you."

Honey lays her head in my lap and I stroke the strands of her pink wig back out of her face and off her shoulders.

"I'm the leader of Pack Star. There's me, Honey, Lucy, Tara, and Sauvignon."

My eyes narrow at the mention of Sauvignon.

"What? You don't like Sauvignon."

"I think Sepp is in love with her," I whisper like it's a secret.

"I think Sepp is in love with you."

"No."

"Yes."

"Hm." I continue to stroke Honey's wig, and she closes her eyes.

I'd love a pack. It's all my inner omega dreams of. How lucky would I be for being asked to be courted by five sexy beta women. There's no way I'd let them go.

That being said, I wouldn't want to leave a certain kind hearted alpha. Once omegas are in a pack, they don't need handlers. However, without an alpha, we couldn't be really bonded.

All of us would make a good pack...together.

"Could I say that you have to court me and Sepp?"

"Would your clan allow that?"

"I'm an omega. I can't be denied."

Carmen smiles at me with a big wide grin, showing off some teeth gems I didn't know she had.

"Do you think I can convince Sepp?" I ask, dreams of the two of us kissing and sleeping together dance through my mind. If he's not in love with me now, maybe I can woo him.

"Sweet Thing, I saw the way he held your hand out there, you have nothing to convince. He's head over heels for you. It's what got me so wet, and I had to find Honey and get off immediately."

I don't even know how to process that information.

I run my knuckles over Honey's cheeks. I don't want to ruin her makeup, but she's letting me pet her and I want to touch her. My touch is relaxing to her too. I like this. I like them.

"Do you want to kiss me?" I ask Carmen.

"I'd love to kiss you." She leans over Honey, and I lean as well, our lips meet. Wow! She's so soft. She opens her mouth and kisses me again, so I do the same. Then I test her with my tongue. We kiss gently like that for a minute, seeing what feels good, letting it get to our heads.

Carmen pulls away, her eyes hooded and her lips plump and kissed.

"Here!" I offer the cash. "For my dance."

"You want a dance, Sweet Thing?"

Honey turns so her back is facing me and puts her arms up on my knees.

While I'm trying to move her hair so it's not trapped between us, Carmen gets some music playing, and then starts her dance.

She turns to me, and I marvel at her stunning body and face. She has orange lips the same color as her hair. I hope we get to make out again.

We are in a great position for her dance to also involve Honey. She leans over us, kissing Honey and then licking me. She shakes her ass in my face and Honey reaches up to kiss her inner thigh.

My dick is hard again, and I'm so worried I'll come in my pants.

"You can take it out, Monroe," Carmen tells me as she grinds in rhythm over my thigh. All I can see is her belly button piercing. My hand is on my cock holding it tight through my jeans.

I should take it out.

Honey helps me undo my belt and take down my jeans a little. I am too tense to take it out of my underwear, so I pull up the band and look at Honey, eyes pleading for her to take the last step.

She dives right in with a lot of enthusiasm.

Carmen also has the same look of excitement.

When she's got it in her hand and it's finally out, I close my eyes tight, unable to be courageous enough to see their reactions. Carmen's body moves away from mine.

"Fuck."

Does that mean they like it or hate it?

Suddenly, I feel two hot mouths on my cock and my eyes fly open. Both girls are between my legs, licking either side of my cock.

"Goodness!" I shout and grab onto them. They moan and sigh, licking my member.

"You taste so good, Monroe. Your cock is everything. So good."

"You like my cock?" I ask, pathetically.

"Oh, yes, baby, it's perfect. It's going to feel so good inside of me."

Honey dips down and sucks my balls into her mouth.

"Fuck! Fuck! Oh my god, Honey, that is amazing."

Girls licking your cock is so much better than alphas. When alphas do it, it's like a race, while this is part of the beta's dance.

With her beautiful long fingers, Carmen strokes my cock, now wet from their mouths.

"Oh wow, Monroe. I see what you've been hiding, you beautiful man," Carmen pants and then takes the head into her mouth. I hold the back of her neck, practically in tears, and then she sucks me down.

She works me up and down, and then my hips meet her. It's warm and tight. I want to get down her throat. I need it.

"I need it, Carmen. I need it more! More! Deeper."

She sucks and then swallows so I'm now in her throat.

"Fuck yes! Fuck! You are just my type, Carmen. God, it's killing me!"

Honey's finger slides down into my pants and plays with the ring of muscle between my ass cheeks.

"I'm going to come!" I shout a warning.

Carmen opens her throat, releasing me, and then comes up to say, "No! I want to fuck you. Can I fuck you? I'm dripping wet. Please."

I'm undone.

I hold her face with one hand, and look into her beautiful amber eyes.

"Anything for you. I'm yours. Anything."

Honey moves out of the way and pulls Carmen's thong down her strong legs and over her tall pink shoes.

Carmen straddles me in the chair, and I grab her hips, helping guide her down on my leaking cock.

Just as her wet pussy touches the tip, I realize this will be my first time with a woman. She's the perfect woman. I'm glad I waited.

"Carmen, how old are you?" I ask, knowing this is a terrible time for that.

"I'm 23."

"I'm 21."

I want to ask her more, but I lose my ability to speak. She smiles and then gives her pussy over to me.

I hold on to her round ass, and fling my head back.

"Carmen, oh my god!" I think I manage to say.

"It's good, isn't it? You and I, we go together."

From this position, her breasts are right in my face. I lick the underside of her nipple, and she moans.

I'm going to come before I even get my cock bounced on.

"You're going to need to move, Carmen. I need you to move."

She huffs out a small breath and then does just that. Leaning forward until I'm nearly out and then falling back down.

Fuck me!

Honey curls over us, and I reach out to touch her too. I'm able to grab her hip and move her into us at the same beat.

Carmen fucks me, I lick her nipple, and Honey moves with us.

"I'm close," Carmen says. Oh my god, is she going to come on my cock?

"Carmen, if you come on my cock, oh my God, I'll fucking die. Please. Please come on my cock. I want that. Please."

She cries out and then so do I. Triggered by her orgasm—I have my own.

I press my face between her breasts and wipe my tears with her skin. She's mine. I just know it.

We stay still like that for a while, panting and catching our breaths. I think they feel exactly how I feel. Like this is the best thing to ever happen to us. That this is good and right between us.

There's a knock at the door and all three of our heads turn to look at it.

"Honey, Carmen, times up. They want you back out there."

I growl. I don't want time to be up.

The girls stand up and put themselves together, then pull me off the chair and fix my hair and clothes for me. I pick up the pile of cash and stand there, not knowing what to do next.

Honey unties her bra and the two little hearts fall into her hand.

"Let's trade."

We trade the money for the top. It's the best thing I've ever exchanged money for in my life!

"Wow!"

She leans over, and we kiss on the lips.

Electricity surges through me. I grab her by the waist and I deepen the kiss. She tastes like honey...

"Mmm coconut. I think we were made for each other," Honey says, almost so casually I don't get to ask why she says that.

Chapter 10

Sepp

I smell him and two beta women behind this door. The music makes it hard to hear anything. But the smell is enough to know he is exceptionally horny and has come at least once.

That's a good thing...

I'm fighting the urge to break the door down and tell him that I love him, too.

I walk back out to the main room, pumping my hand in and out of a fist. Monroe confessed his feelings for me, and they are the same as mine. I don't want him thinking we don't have the same feelings any longer than necessary.

I was just lost in my own head, and he was being impatient. A trait I've grown fond of from him.

Sauvignon pours someone a drink at the bar, and I walk up. She smiles brightly at me.

"Sepp! You made it! Where did your omega go?" she shouts over the music.

"He's in a private room."

"Oh! With my Stars!?"

"I think so!"

She laughs and jumps up and down, her hands in little fists. She was really hoping, *that much*, that her pack mates would like Monroe? This is really happening, isn't it?! She slides over a shot of clear liquor and holds its twin in her hand.

"Take a shot with me!"

I take it gladly, and we both shoot what turns out to be tequila.

"Woo!" I yell at the burn. She pours me another and I take that too.

When I drink I become quite the manwhore. This is the place for that, so I ask for another one. I'm also a big guy, so I can take it.

She laughs at me and then turns to take the next drink order from the cute blonde, Tara. She listens to the drinks, but then grabs her waist and pulls her in, whispering in her ear. Tara is cute as hell. She has yellow hair tied half up, and scheming eyes. Her sweet little outfit is begging to get ruined.

She asks Sauvignon if she's sure a few times, then they kiss on the mouth, and she slaps her ass. Tara comes over shyly.

Shy like Monroe.

Tara is a little nervous around alphas, I bet.

I dip my chin and hide my hands, something I used to do for Monroe when I first became his handler. I used to scare him too.

I think he gets nervous when he likes someone.

She comes up, her eyes darting about.

"Do you need anything, Sepp? While you wait?"

Her beautiful eyes finally stick the landing up at me with earnest. I move slowly so my mouth is closer to her ear.

"Yeah, maybe somewhere quiet?" I tell her and feel her shiver.

Oh, she's going to be fun.

Tara takes my wrist and pulls me away from the bar, Sauvignon gives her a wink, and we rush away.

She takes me down another hallway that has a line of private rooms. We make our way further and further down until we come up to one with a green light above it, and she rushes in.

I'm worked up from watching the dancers. My body is hot from seeing Sauvignon again. My heart is pounding from imagining Monroe getting his cock sucked by two beautiful beta women. So, when Tara and I get into the room, I take her and slam her against the wall, and kiss her. I press my hips into her, making her very aware of my hard cock, and my hands grab both of her breasts over her lacy top.

She moans.

Thank fuck.

It's a sweet moan, and I eat it up, driving my tongue into her. When Sauvignon slapped her ass earlier, I took it as a sign Tara wouldn't mind being manhandled. It was a safe bet. She's chasing everything I do to her. I drive my knee between her legs, and she opens up to me.

Her hands go into my hair and she hoists herself up off her feet, balancing between my knee and the wall.

I slide my hand to her back and pull her right into me. She squeaks, and I grin over her lips.

"Tell me if you don't like something, Precious. I can make adjustments."

"Harder," she breathes.

I kiss her neck, then suck in some of the delicate skin. She cries out.

"Can I fuck you?" I ask.

"Please, please, please. I want that big, alpha cock. I want it so bad, Sepp."

I kiss her hard, and she whimpers again.

"Tell me, Tara, how do you feel about me and Monroe?" I ask over her lips.

"I'm excited," she pants. "We want an omega, and he's really cute." I growl and then suck in her nipple. "Sauvignon came home so happy. She's already got a therapy appointment. Which is so big for her."

Therapy? I wonder why Sauvignon needs therapy.

I pop out her ripe, wet nipple from my mouth.

"Is she ok?"

"Our old boss, who was sort of her boyfriend, got eaten by a tiger."

I stop.

"What?"

"Legs O'Bannon. I'm sure you heard about it. Sauvignon found him. He died in the hospital a few weeks afterwards."

I guess I do remember hearing about a clan leader dying by an illegally owned tiger. That was big news last year.

"Sauvignon and him...?"

"It wasn't a good relationship. He was an evil man. She's been messed up about it. I think she's processing their whole relationship. But she's already doing better."

Tara said he was their employer. Meaning, none of them were in a good situation.

"My clan, Clan Foxx, will take good care of you. Their clan leader..."

"He's your uncle, isn't he?"

"How did you know?"

"I like to know things. I already looked you two up."

I smile.

"You know everyone's secrets?"

"Yes, I do."

"Tell me what you know about me and Monroe then?"

I am still touching and feeling her; she reaches down and pulls her thong to one side, and without missing a beat, I unbuckle my belt, undo my pants, and take out my cock, pressing the tip to her entrance.

"I know the clan leader is your uncle. He's also tight with the mayor, but not in a corrupt official way, more like they do city projects together. Clan Foxx took over the care of Monroe when his parents died. I'm guessing it's so he will choose a clan member to bond. That's you, isn't it? They want you to bond?"

I stop and look her in the eyes.

"I don't think so."

She looks down at my cock pressing into her and whimpers. I ease it in slightly.

"Why else would they have an unbonded alpha like you become his handler?" she asks. I press into her more. "He looks at you like you hung the moon, Sepp. You two were set up. You didn't like anyone else, did you?"

Like the sun is finally peeking over the horizon, it all makes sense. My uncle asked me many times if I scented anyone special, or if I met anyone I liked. I just thought he was interested in romance stories, not that he was particularly interested in mine. I told him I liked Monroe's coconut scent.

Tara pushes her hips into me, getting more of my cock inside her. I stop teasing her and give her what she wants, all of me. I fuck her against the wall and recall the time when my uncle asked me to be his handler.

"Monroe wants to go to school and hasn't found a bonded alpha yet," he said to me.

"Do you want me to be his handler while he goes to school? I can make sure he is safe and no one bothers him while he finds his pack."

I remember the funny look he gave me, and then a smile like he was laughing at me as he said, "Sure, yeah, you can be his handler. Let's see how that goes."

Was I even assigned as his handler, or did I assume...

"Oh my god," I say out loud here with Tara. She says it too, as I ramp up my speed, fucking her harder and harder.

Tara holds my forearms for support, but I don't stop.

"Monroe wouldn't have been happy with just me, though. I knew his type, and it wasn't large alpha males. It's you. Beta women..."

She's so wet, and I can't stop. I never want to stop fucking her wet pussy.

"I think you won him over. He told you he loved you out there—I heard him. And you brought him to us. You're a good alpha, Sepp. Look at what you do for those you love." She can talk while getting fucked. That's not good. I need to try a lot harder. I want to render her speechless.

Then she says, with a quiet voice I can barely hear over the pounding of the music on the other side of the door, "I'd like to be loved like that one day."

My attention all pools to her.

"You seem really easy to love."

I get deeper and harder, to show her I'm serious. I pull her hips into me, fucking her as full as I can so she is bumping into my knot at the base of my cock. Knotting betas can be done, but only if they are nice and ready.

"We made an offer to another omega once, Aurora, but she didn't really like me. She said I was a busybody and seemed exhausted by me."

Her words are laced with vulnerability. I slow down, then reach down to touch her clit.

"Tara, Monroe would never. He loves everyone, and he treats people so well. He would cherish you. I would cherish you if you'd let me. He was so nervous coming out tonight I thought he was going to run. He thinks of you as little goddesses already, and I doubt that would ever change."

She seems convinced about Monroe, but I want her to be sure about both of us.

"Tara, should I prove it to you?"

"How?"

"I'll bite you. Right now. We could bond."

"What!?"

"Do you want to be first?"

"I don't know..."

"It's best if we bond while fucking. That's the strongest bond."

"Shouldn't I get Carmen's permission?"

"If you'd like. Or I can, and we can get it started."

"You want to bond me?!"

"I'm going to need to bite six people, so should we get started?"

"You are insane."

I feel sane. I dip down and run my sharp teeth over her neck. Normally I wouldn't be this overt, but she brings it out of me. I've been thinking about bonding ever since Sauvignon. I'm ready. I've never been more sure. Alphas have a tendency to be confident in their choices, and I'm so damned confident.

"It won't hurt. I'll make it feel real good."

She moans and I dig my teeth in even more, not breaking the skin, just giving her a taste. I keep fucking her pussy, so she knows I can multitask.

"Stop, Sepp. Stop. I get your point. You should bite Monroe first. He's an omega, he will be hurt if he isn't first."

"You're so smart, Tara. I'm going to keep you close. I can't wait to get my teeth into you while I rut inside your warm, wet pussy."

I circle her clit and fuck her pussy until I feel her get close, and I don't stop until she can no longer speak. I whisper things to her about what I would do to her. How much I like her. How beautiful she is. She comes on my cock like a good little beta.

I let her down onto her feet, help her find her balance, then we rush out to find Monroe. I hold her hand tight. I'm not letting Tara go.

Chapter 11

Monroe

I don't see Sepp immediately, and I panic. Did he leave me?! Is he mad at me? I'm standing in the club with two beautiful women hanging off me on either side, looking around desperately for my alpha.

What is my life?

Finally, I see him with a bright, glowing face, leading that pretty blonde beta through the crowd. He's got a smile so big it shows all his teeth. That only happens when he's been drinking.

I bet he spent some time with Sauvignon at the bar.

He comes up to me and, before stopping, pulls me up and into a hug, bringing my feet off the ground.

"Monroe," he says close to my ear, and I go limp in his arms. This is lovely. A purr bubbles up in my chest. "Did you have a nice time with your Stars?"

My Stars?!

"Sepp, I'm having the best time of my entire life actually," I say. "They really liked my cock!"

"I knew they would."

He gives me a tight squeeze, then sets me down.

I don't like that he let me go. He smiles at my pouting face.

A man in casual clothes comes up to my Stars and reminds them that they are both working.

"And unless these are paying customers, the three of you can't be gathered here. We have a full house tonight, ladies."

Sepp growls low in his chest, but I just reach deep into his pants pocket and pull out his cash, flashing it across the space between us.

"They aren't here for just my good looks, sir," I say with the most confidence I've ever had. Sepp is shocked by my audacity and is at a loss for words.

Carmen wraps her arms around my shoulders and reaffirms to their manager she knows what she's doing. Honey moves in front of me and opens up her strap on her thong, so I put some bills there. She grabs my hand before I can pull it away and brings it up to her mouth, sucking my thumb into her mouth.

I'm pretty sure Honey is the freakiest person I know. I'll never tire of her freak.

"Ok, ok, I get it. Take them to the VIP area and have a fun night. I'll get someone else to dance."

He bows slightly to Sepp, then to me, finally, he leaves.

Carmen takes my hand, holding it above our heads, and walks us to the VIP section.

Passing by all the other patrons, surrounded by not one but three of the most beautiful girls here, and followed by the handsome alpha, I feel powerful. Why was I ever worried? Their presence and attention invigorates me.

I catch the eye of the guy from earlier who told me Carmen was only teasing me. I nod towards Carmen, and wag my eyebrows.

He still has that look on his face–like he thinks I'm being fooled.

I stop, yank Carmen back, spinning her into me and bring my lips close to hers.

"Can I kiss you?"

The rest of our group stops too.

"Of course, Sweet Thing."

I dip her down and give her one hell of a kiss. She melts in my arms, and when I pop her back up she looks a little dazed. Then I look back at the guy, who finally looks shocked.

I'm a fucking omega. I think. Everyone here either wants to fuck me, or be me.

Carmen takes my hand again, and we get to the VIP area.

It's a loft area looking down at the main stage, but it also has its own pole in the middle of a half moon couch.

Sepp sits down on the couch and brings me into his lap, and it surprises the hell out of me. He pulls Tara close on his other side. She looks up at me through her gorgeous, long eyelashes.

"Hi," she says, and I give her a little wave. It's so dorky, I can't even believe that just happened. She waves back.

Sepp gives me a little squeeze.

They announce the next dancer.

"Welcome to the stage for the first time, the beautiful, the enigmatic, the talented...Sauvignon Star!"

Sepp sits up a little straighter, and we look down at the stage to Sauvignon, strutting around a pole, teasing it.

Tara gasps. Carmen and Honey whistle loudly and cheer.

Tara leans over and tells us, "She hasn't danced since her boyfriend got eaten by a tiger! Sauv taught most of us to pole dance. She's the best! This is amazing!"

A tiger? I want to ask a follow up question, but I'm rendered speechless.

Sepp's attention is all on her dance, so I follow his line of sight. She scales the pole and clacks her heels together, then while upside down she removes her gold top, letting it fall to the stage, and revealing her large breasts. She's wearing star pasties on her nipples. Then she flies off the pole, landing in the splits, immediately bouncing her ass. It makes the whole crowd pay attention to her.

She flips around and shakes her thighs, clacks her heels, then whips her hair. It's her eye contact that elevates her dance. Even watching her make eye contact with other people in the crowd is exciting.

Honey whistles again. People toss money onto the stage.

She's a great dancer, and when she's done, she joins us in the VIP area. We spend the night laughing, drinking, and messing around. The Stars take turns on the small pole we have up here to show off their skills, dance to their favorite songs that play, or cheer on the other dancers on the main stage. Sepp, at one point, pulls me under him and we make out on the couch.

He whispers in my ear, "I love you too, Monroe. I've loved you for a long time. You're mine."

I grab his face and make him look at me.

"Say it again."

"I love you, baby."

Barely coherent at the end of the night, the Stars take us back to their apartment which is nearby. We didn't bring a car so we are more than happy to be taken home. It's a spectacular downtown loft. They get us beers and take turns showering, never leaving us alone, and we continue to talk about everything; Our thoughts on what's happening in the news. Our favorite movies. Funny things about their neighbors. Everything. Sepp never lets go of my hand. The sun will be rising soon, and without too much convincing, Carmen asks us to get in bed with them.

"To sleep," she says, and I think she means it.

I take off my clothes, leave on my underwear, and join them. It's Tara, Sepp, me, Carmen, and Honey, in that order in their very large bed.

But I know someone is missing.

They said that Lucy was working the night shift at the Pinched Rose. I can't sleep knowing there's one more beta girl, and she's missing. While most of them are pretty much asleep, I slip out from between Sepp and Carmen.

The hallway is dark, but it doesn't scare me. Honestly, Carmen was right when she told us that this place is very relaxing. It smells lovely, like honeycomb and lavender. My coconut and Sepp's apricot go very well with their subtle beta smells.

There's only two bedrooms here. The one everyone is piled into and one they kept close the whole time we were winding down.

I walk over to the other bedroom door and try turning the handle. It opens easily. I wondered if it would be locked.

Tara's lavender scent and someone else's scent...I close my eyes and breathe in until my head is woozy. Mulberry! That's the scent that's most prominent here.

I open my eyes and in the darkness I start to make out what looks like a movie studio. The northern facing windows reveal the rising sun, and the light slowly brightens the room.

There are tripods, backdrops, and a wall of whips, leather belts, masks, ball gags...

This room looks familiar...

I find myself standing in the middle looking at the dancer's pole, then looking around. The purple chair and leather footstool are alarmingly familiar...

Oh my god.

This is the set for the femme domme I subscribe to online.

This is the Superstar BDSM Playroom!

The door opens, and standing there is Lucy herself.

I didn't put it together.

This is the beta woman who does kinky scenes, and I watch *all* of them. She's wearing a black trench coat tied tightly around her waist and is holding two black thigh-high boots in her hands. She must have just come back from her shift at the sex toy shop.

I recognize her with that same short black hair and black lipstick. She wears masks in her videos, but here she is—exposed.

She's stunning.

It's intimidating, but in the kind of way that makes me hard.

"Lucy?" I ask. Just to make sure I'm not dreaming.

"You're Monroe, the omega."

"Yes, that's right. Also...I know you." I gesture to the room.

"Oh." Her eyes dart to her wall of whips. "You've seen my videos."

I'm not sure how she feels about that. She delivers the line with no emotion. She could be tired from working all night at The Pinched Rose. But something tells me she is hesitant to reveal her emotions until she knows mine.

"I've seen all your videos. I didn't know you were part of Pack Star."

"Oh, you subscribe to different channels..."

"No, just yours. Just yours," I rush to say.

She takes a deep breath, then walks into the room, closer to me.

"You've seen all of my videos?"

I swallow hard.

She looks so much sexier in real life. Her eyes see right into me. In the videos I can look away, but here in real life, she has me in a trance.

"I like the ones where you and..." I'm thinking about the video where she has a blonde woman tied up and gagged and she fucks her with a fat dildo until she's crying and begging to come...

"Tara. It's you and Tara."

She nods.

"I'm realizing something," I say just as she gets close enough to touch her chest to mine.

"What, Pretty Omega?"

I can only breathe out, not in.

"I like the videos because I can tell Tara trusts you, and you really love her."

The way she takes care of her sub is so much more than anything I'd ever come across. Lucy wipes her tears, and listens to all her cues, and goes the extra mile in her after-care—telling her such sweet things and massaging her whole body. She always tests Tara's fingers and toes to make sure she isn't pushing her too hard...

"I enjoy watching you care for her. That's my favorite part."

The sun is rising more and the room fills with a beautiful pink light. Her face becomes more clear to me.

"You have freckles," I say and raise my hand to touch her cheek, but pause until she nods for me to continue.

I rest my hand on her cheek and stroke the freckles.

"I do love Tara. She was the first one I fell for. Honey next, then Carmen and Sauvignon. I love them more than anything."

"And you want an omega? I have an alpha, too. Can you love two more?"

She rests her hand on top of mine. It's so delicate, but I know what her hands can do.

"Yes," is all she replies. I want to know her reasons, and yet I can tell I will have to earn those answers.

"I think I'd love to be loved by you. It would be glorious," I whisper.

She looks into my eyes like she's looking for something deep inside of me.

"I like to be in charge during sex," she says, but it's more like a question. She's asking if I would be ok with that.

"If you take care of me like you take care of Tara, I think it will be fine."

"Show me."

"What?"

"Show me you can be a good sub."

All my blood runs through my body like there's a crisis it needs to attend to but doesn't know where.

The air in the room is thick with lust and possibility. I'm not normally adventurous, and I spook easily, but I trust this woman. I've seen how she takes care of her subs.

"Where do you want me, Lucy?"

Chapter 12

Sepp

I smell my omega climaxing.

The scent takes me right out of my deep sleep. Sauvignon holds me tight, making me the little spoon, and there's an empty spot in the bed in front of me where Monroe should be. Where is that man?

I slowly sit up, but my size makes it hard to go unnoticed. Also, I can hear moaning and crying from somewhere else in the apartment.

The five of us sit up, too. Sunshine filters into the room. It's probably only been a few hours since we laid down.

"Is that..." Sauvignon asks, and Carmen answers, "That's Lucy and Monroe."

Lucy! The missing Star.

Carmen puts her hand on my arm.

"Are you ok?"

"There's just...a lot of you."

She laughs, and Honey lifts off her silk mask to roll her eyes at me.

"I need to go check on him."

I get out of bed and adjust the waistband of my underwear. All four pairs of their eyes go to the movement. I look down, and sure enough, I have a half staff.

"It gets bigger," I say.

"Oh, I know," Tara sighs.

I shake my head and then turn to leave; they get out of bed behind me, following me to where I smell my omega. His coconut and her mulberry scent really play well together. The door to this other room is ajar, and I push it open to find quite a scene.

Monroe is on all fours, wearing a collar, and has his head buried between Lucy's thighs. She's laying down, and has her foot on his cock, covered in cum, and her head is thrown back in ecstasy. They are on some large round black cushion big enough for many people, maybe even all of us.

It kind of looks like an omega nest.

This room is not really a room. It's a sex dungeon. There's whips, chains, collars and everything else a domme might need for sex play. There's also a camera tripod, though nothing is on it.

Lucy is close. She doesn't mind our presence, if anything, she's going to come sooner because of it.

I note that she let Monroe come first. He must have been very well behaved.

Sauvignon stands next to me and I take her hand, and she leans her head against my arm, warming my insides up. Watching my omega eat out a beta woman like it's the only thing in the world he wants to do, is so beautiful. I knew this was right the minute Sauvignon mentioned her pack. Tara stands at my other side, so I put my arm around her.

Lucy comes, crying out Monroe's name.

He kisses her thighs and stomach, working his way up to her mouth where they finally kiss on the mouth.

She puts her hands on his face and says, "You were such a good boy. You are so good at that. What do you want as your reward?"

Monroe turns his head to see the rest of us.

He considers each one of us, then his eyes stay on mine.

"A bite. A bite from Sepp."

Omegas never hold back when they want something. I'm going to bite him, bond him, and then if the Stars want him they'll get me, too. I won't let him back out now.

Nothing is holding me back.

I climb into the big cushion and pick him up off of Lucy, bringing him into my lap, then put my mouth on his chest.

"Yes, please Sepp. Bite me."

"This is forever, baby. You know that, right?"

He nods furiously. He reaches up and removes his collar and Lucy takes it from him.

"Yes. I want it."

Carmen, Honey, Tara, and Sauvignon join us, too. They surround us like the five points of a star. I open my jaws and breathe in his lovely scent. The coconut scent I've had the privilege of surrounding myself with for the last year.

"Oh Monroe, are you really going to be mine?"

"Yes. Yes. Yes. And Pack Star, please.."

I look over at Sauvignon who smiles warmly at me.

"I love that you are all here with us. This feels right."

"We should be next," Honey says. They're right, Honey always has the best ideas.

"Sepp, do you think Clan Foxx will be upset?"

I lick his skin, right where I'm planning to bite him.

"I thought so, but Tara let me know I may have had things wrong."

Tara giggles and Honey hugs her.

"Clan Foxx set you two up," she says.

Monroe makes a cute noise like he's realizing what I did earlier, that we were always going to end up like this.

"Omega Monroe, I promise to be a good alpha for you. I'll strive to always take good care of you, and I promise you my devotion. I'm yours entirely." His chest is rumbling with an intense purr. "You ready?" I ask, then press my sharp alpha teeth into his skin.

"Yes, Alpha. Bite me. Bond me."

It's so perfect that his beta harem is here to witness. I press his back into me, and then bite down hard. His yelp turns into a moan. My bite is a request, and screaming through my mouth is his response—Yes! Suddenly we're connected by some otherworldly thing. All his emotions drop next to mine. I find we aren't much different at all.

Horny. Excited. Tired. Hopeful. And absolutely in love.

I extract my teeth and then lick the wound as it drips dark, life changing blood down Monroe's heaving chest.

My omega.

Mine.

"Sepp, knot me, please. I want a knot."

I lay him down on his back, but his hips are still up in my lap. I'm hard as a rocket ship about to take off into the stratosphere, so there's no need to get myself ready. I stroke him between his legs, over his cock and balls, and then down between his ass. Omegas slick their ass when they are turned on, and Monroe is definitely turned on. I test him with my fingers, and loosen him up.

"Oh my god, Sepp!" he cries out. I piston my fingers in, slowly, then more quickly, opening him up, getting him ready for me. Monroe reaches out to his Stars, and grabs onto Lucy and Honey. Lucy, takes Tara and guides her over Monroe's face.

"Are you going to be a good boy and show Tara what I taught you?"

"Yes," Monroe whimpers so pathetically.

Tara straddles Monroe's face at the same time Lucy grabs Monroe's cock and gives it a stroke.

"Fuck!" he cries out but then snuffs it out with meeting Tara's cunt halfway, burying his face in her.

I pull my fingers out and then line my cock up with his asshole. I have to do some adjusting, but soon, I'm ready to start pushing myself inside. Sauvignon strokes my back, which has broken out into a sweat, and lays her bare breasts into my side as I push further and further into Monroe.

He cries out against Tara's pussy. She also cries out, and Lucy sits up to kiss her, letting go of Monroe's cock.

I'm fully inside of him, my heart is beating wildly, and the room is filling more and more with the haze of lust.

I'm going to lose it.

"Come on, Alpha. Fuck him," Carmen insists.

That's all I need to break. I grab Monroe's hips and fuck him. It makes his face slide back and forth against Tara and both of them love it. Monroe feels incredible surrounding me.

We work together and get lost in the rut of it all. They are enjoying it, touching us, making their own sounds of pleasure, and my eyes are right on my bond mark. I lean down, pressing his leaking cock between us, and put my mouth over the fresh bond mark.

Tara comes first, crying out into Lucy's mouth, then Monroe comes between us. I sit up and rub his cum all over his stomach, then fuck him until I come.

Then I push my knot inside of him, trapping us both together.

"Fuck!" We all cry out on our own.

Tara has to be lifted off of Monroe, and she crumbles to the side, hand on her omega. Honey looks so worked up and is staring right at Monroe's growing cock.

"Do you think I could climb on top, Monroe? I could fuck your cock while your alpha is knotted in your ass?"

Monroe looks at her like she hung the moon.

"Yes, please, Honey. Yes. Yes Yes. Yes."

I help Honey straddle Monroe, with her ass in my lap. Monroe has to spread his legs wide, but the girls help him do that without pulling a muscle. Honey takes my hands and places them on her body.

She has a great body. Her hands rub Monroe's chest, and her finger nails scrape the skin. Finally, she sinks down onto Monroe's cock. I take Honey's breasts in my hands and tease her ripe nipples.

Then I stay out of her way as she fucks the omega.

She's trying to get herself off, and I've never experienced anything this erotic in my life. Every crash of her ass into our lap, makes my cock move inside of him and it's going to make me come again while I'm inside of him!

Honey knows what she's doing. She gets herself, and the two of us off with her bouncing.

I feel so close to death. It's wonderful. Monroe is off this planet, I'm pretty sure.

And he's not done. Once Honey demounts, Monroe is getting hard again. I look through my hazy eyes and see him watching Sauvignon. Their eye contact is intense.

"Should each Star take a turn on your cock, Monroe?" I ask with my gravelly voice.

He nods, not taking his eyes off of Sauvignon.

"Sauvignon next," he says.

She shivers with pleasure, and then straddles Monroe. She leans forward, putting her breasts in his face, and I help guide his cock inside of her very wet pussy.

He latches onto her nipple, and she fucks him. I hold onto her ass, grateful to be involved.

Monroe comes with Sauvignon, Carmen, and then Lucy before my knot relaxes, and I slip out. He jumps up and crashes into Tara, then mounts her on top. She giggles, and then cries out as he fucks her hard into the pillows. They pull me into a pile and hold me while Monroe fucks his little beta.

I wish I was still inside of him.

Later, when we are holding each other in a tight pile, about to drift off to sleep again, my cheek pressed into Monroe's chest, I ask the question burning in my mind.

"When will you all be ready?" I ask.

"Let us court the omega properly before the bite," Carmen says softly, and the rest of them nod. "We've been waiting a long time to do this. Let us spoil him and fall in love with both of you."

"Of course. And it'll give me time to change my name."

"What?"

"What do you think of Sepp Star? Too obvious?"

When an alpha bonds a pack they are known as his last name. I don't want to bond them and be known as Pack Seppton.

We are Pack Star.

Tara laughs loudly, thrown off from my announcement. Lucy joins her.

Sauvignon opens her eyes to see me staring back at her.

"Are you serious?"

She's so beautiful. I kiss her instead of answering.

Of course I'm serious. They are special, and they decided on their pack name long before I came around. Who am I to demand they carry my name?

Epilogue

Sauvignon

About six weeks after we met Monroe, he's about to go into heat. About five weeks and six days ago, he asked us to join him in his heat.

He's the cutest thing that we've ever had around, giving Tara a run for her money.

He wants it at his place with Sepp, but he just arrived at our loft because he wants to borrow some of our things for his nest.

Monroe bursts through the front door like a bird that's fallen into a hole. If he had wings, which by all accounts it feels like he has wings, he'd by fluttering them around chaotically, knocking over small tables and tripping over floor cushions. Carmen rushes to grab him, to make him be still. Sepp is behind him holding bags and other items, including a pizza.

Thank god, I'm hungry as sin.

Sepp is so good to us. He always feels the need to feed us, and I've gotten very used to it. Now, I just wait until I see him again to eat. It's a bad habit, but he's so damned reliable.

I knew he was Monroe's handler, but finding out how much caregiving he does is shocking. He insists on being our driver, cook, cleaner, seamstress, and more. We aren't used to this much support, but he is like a force that we can't stop.

Monroe is used to this level of care.

He's just not used to the attention us Stars give him.

I swear he's blushed nearly the entire 6-weeks we've been courting him.

He and Tara are really close. They have so many things in common. I swear they can read each other's thoughts by now. They play the same RPG games, watch the same romance shows, and are very submissive in bed, much to the delight of Lucy. She now has two dedicated subs. Neither of which are brats, like Honey and I can be. Lucy is a good brat tamer, but there's something so special about a domme having subs that turn into putty in her hands immediately.

Then there's Honey and Sepp.

They've established a "free-use" situation between them. So, at any time, without first checking in, Honey can sexually attack Sepp. I guess he can do it back, but she is the one that takes advantage all the time. She wakes him up with his cock in her mouth constantly. She joins him in the shower. She strokes him over the pants while he's driving...

They have a safe word and I've learned it is not "Oh my god Honey, not now!" and it's not "fucking, fuck, fuck, I think people can see!"

Carmen and I have gotten closer again, like at the old Pack House, but this time instead of it being because we shared the same master, we are simply each other's best friend.

My therapist was worried about us being too reliant on each other, and has told me that we need to have our own hobbies, but come together at the end of the day as one.

So, in an effort to continue on my healing journey, I've decided to start teaching pole dance.

I teach three times a week at a local place, and have over fifty students. It's become a huge part of my life. My therapist asks about it every session with a huge smile on her face. I could spend the whole session talking about my classes.

Carmen–along with Honey–has enrolled at cosmetology school.

I've never seen her more hopeful than when she came back from her tour with Monroe and Sepp with all of her pamphlets. Honey enrolled right alongside her. Sepp drives them to class even though it's completely out of his way.

I take the pizza from Sepp and he leans in for a kiss. I give him a quick one, because hunger has consumed me, and I bring the pizza to the counter and dive in.

Because of Monroe's heat, I've had to cancel classes for the next week, and some of my students asked for private lessons today so they don't miss out. That's where I've been all morning.

With my mouth full of chicken, bacon, and hot honey pizza, I turn to see the flighty bird omega. He appears to be searching earnestly for something. He's down on the ground, crawling around, looking under chairs and couches. His head pops up near my legs and I see his red-rimmed, wet eyes and crestfallen face.

"Oh my god, Monroe, is everything ok?"

He smiles, but it cracks, and tears fall down his face, and instead of answering me he goes back to looking around. His hand dives into the couch cushions and pulls out some panties. Mine. He rubs them across his lips, then sits back. Sepp runs up with one of the bags and opens it up, and Monroe deposits the panties.

"Wait, what is happening?" I ask.

"He's really hormonal. It's nothing to worry about," Sepp explains. "His nest isn't right. He needs your scents. So, we're here to get the things he needs to add to his nest."

Oh my god.

He needs my panties for his nest!

He finds Carmen's panties too, in the same spot. We didn't clean up last night when we were messing around. Whoops.

He puts those in the bag too. While me and the rest of the Stars eat pizza, we watch the chaotic omega fumble around the house lifting panties, thongs, bras, fishnets, nylons, socks, and then shoving them into the bag. He finally makes it to our east facing window and sees the clothesline with all of our clean delicate things hanging in the sun.

He stands there completely still, and when he turns around, more tears wet his cheeks.

"Why are they all clean! They smell like laundry detergent! They smell nothing like you!" he cries.

I'm remembering Sepp when I first met him at the Pinched Rose and he told me he thought Monroe was mad at him. I think this is exactly what that was. Monroe is angry at us!

Lucy steps in, thank god, and saunters over to the wet, messy omega.

"Little rabbit, tell me what you need."

He whimpers.

"Use your words."

"Cocoa." His head falls forward, defeated. "Honey. Mulberry. Lavender." He looks up at me, and says, desperately, "Cinnamon."

He doesn't break eye contact.

I gulp.

Having his attention makes me feel so undeserving. He has Sepp. He has the rest of the Stars. When he gives me his attention it makes me wonder what I did to win the attention of someone so special.

I know after his heat that we will be connected by more than our shared desire, but by some otherworldly thing, because Sepp wants to fuck each of us and then bite us. He's brought it up almost every time I'm fucking him. He nips at my skin with his sharp alpha teeth, and when he does it I nearly come.

"You heard our omega," Lucy says to the rest of us. "Go get him some things so he doesn't have to crawl around the loft. Monroe, come sit down like the prince you are and we will bring you things. And Sepp, you have circles under your eyes so dark I'm afraid they'll become permanent. You sit down too."

Sepp doesn't listen, he just starts going through the bag and making sure everything is accounted for. Lucy marches up to him, takes the bag, and drags him to a seat.

Sepp has barely slept since he's been preparing for a heat for seven people.

"Sauvignon. My name change went through. My uncle and the judge got it signed this morning. I'd been so worried..."

He was worried if he didn't get it done before binding then we'd have legal issues surrounding our pack name. He's such a good man, a good alpha.

"Sepp, my love," I say, and get closer. "That's so wonderful. You worked so hard for us. Now, let us take care of your omega. You're going to need to bite five people in the next couple of days, so take a break. We got it. We'll get all the things packed up."

I lean over and rub his thighs and he looks at me like I hung the moon. I give him a kiss and then pass my hand over his eyes.

"Sleep. Take a little nap. I'll wake you up when he's ready."

His eyes don't open back up.

The Stars and I take Monroe to the bedroom and sit him on the bed, and then each present him with our worn, used clothing. He indicates with a nod or a shake of the head which ones he wants, and the pile grows. When we aren't paying attention, he works the pile into the bedding, like he's possessed by something. He acts like this is a solvable issue. Or he's got a plan. But he keeps moving things around from one place to another.

He makes agreeable noises, frustrated sighs, and grumpy grumbles. Should he be nesting in our bed? Maybe we should get him back to his place.

"Monroe, let's get these things packed away and get you home." I reach into the nest to take one of my shirts, and he growls at me.

I pull my hand back, surprised.

"Oh no, I'm so sorry!" Monroe cries and buries his face in his hands. "I can't believe I growled at you!"

I crawl into the bed and take his wrists, pulling his hands away from his face.

"No, no, no. It's ok. I shouldn't have taken anything."

Monroe grabs me and pulls me closer to him, growling again.

"You can take anything you want from me, Sauv."

His emotions are rotating violently, but I do like this one. His hands are hard on my body and our faces are close.

"Sauvignon?"

"Yes?"

"Sepp told me something," he whispers.

I lean in closer.

"What?"

"He said you teased him with a masturbator machine."

"I did. He ended up fucking me instead."

"Do you have it?" His big blue eyes plead at me.

I can't believe he's asking me about it. The idea they talked about it kind of thrills me, actually. When I went back into the changing room, it was all boxed up, and I actually bought it. I've been wanting to use it on Sepp for some time, but we haven't yet.

"I do."

He whimpers.

"Can you use it on me?" I nod but he doesn't look done. "Just like you wanted to use it on Sepp?"

If I wasn't wet before, I am now. I brush his hair back. His pupils are huge and his mouth is slightly open as he pants. I turn my head to find Honey.

"Honey, go get the Masturbator Megacock30000. The red one. It's still in the box. I left it in the front closet."

"Hell yes."

She leaves and I turn to Monroe, whose skin has broken out in a sweat.

"Sweetheart, are you ok?"

He just answers me with a whine.

I reach down between us and stroke his very hard cock over his pants. He growls and groans and falls into me. I need his pants off, so I use both hands to keep stroking his cock, and remove them. He makes even more sounds: purring, grumbling, sighing, hissing, and moaning.

Frustrated, he grabs me again and buries his nose into my neck, smelling me. When that isn't enough he licks me, like he's trying to get underneath my skin with just his tongue.

He's desperate for my scent.

"It's hot. Like hot cinnamon candy," he says, mostly to himself.

Honey comes back with all the Stars and the box. She takes it out and reads the instructions, and by the time she's done, I finally have Monroe's pants and shirt off.

He stares at my clothes like they've personally offended him. I take the hint and undress, earning me some positive, but still aggressive noises.

I bring the masturbator machine closer to us, then push his chest to get him to lay back on some pillows. Honey takes his legs and spreads them wide. Carmen and Honey join us, and then Lucy.

Each additional girl makes his heart pound faster and his eyes grow wider. We overwhelm him every time and I've grown addicted to it.

Lucy strokes his cock, getting it hard for the machine, and I line it up above him. It's a box with red lights on it. Very masculine and futuristic.

"Ok, Omega, just relax and let your Stars take good care of you."

I bring the machine down over his cock, and turn it on. The sucking and pulling motion pulls his cock inside inch by inch. He shouts and his head flies back, and we watch it suck his cock in. Honey and Carmen stroke his stomach and chest. Lucy bends down along with Tara, and they suck on his neck.

He's finally all the way inside.

My chest is so hot watching this.

I switch the setting, and now it basically milks him with tight, quick strokes. Tighter than a human hand.

"Fuck!" he screams. Carmen and Honey suck and tease his nipples.

I'm bringing this, along with some many more things, to his heat. Why didn't I think of it before?

"More. Please. Oh my god, Sauv, more."

I love how unrelenting he is.

"Lucy? Nipple clamps?"

She laughs and runs out of the room to get them.

"And a butt plug," I shout.

Monroe huffs and puffs underneath me, and my whole job is operating the box, and to wet my inner thighs from the display.

Lucy returns, and Carmen and Honey take their time teasing him and then clamping his nipples. Tara and Lucy pull his knees up, then hand me the lubed up butt plug.

It's in this moment I think we forgot the omega slicks his own ass. We aren't used to the idea that butt stuff doesn't include some serious lube. Well, it can't hurt.

"Yes. Oh my god, yes, Sauv. Please, put it in. Please fuck my ass, Sauv. Spit on it first. I want your scent all over it."

I hand the box holding duties off to Lucy, then lean down, spitting down over his asshole while his thighs are pushed up to the sides.

Then I take the butt plug and gently coax it inside.

"No! No!" Monroe shouts.

I pull it out.

"Sorry."

Tears stream down his face.

"No, I mean, don't be gentle. Fuck me with it! I can take it."

Fine. If that's what the omega wants. I take a breath, then shove it in, hard. I half expect it to go wrong, but he just lets out the most delicious, satisfied moan.

I wish I would have gotten a dildo instead.

Monroe cries out in less ineligible words, and I leave it in, then bring his knees back down.

Lucy switches the machine to the next level.

"I'm going to come!" he warns only seconds before the machine yanks a climax out of him. I switch it off, and it slows down until I turn the motion off, then switch on the heat.

There's a reservoir to catch his cum.

Tears fall down the sides of his head, and he's muttering to himself. The Stars kiss him all over, and he tries his best to touch them, but he's pretty useless right now.

"Sauvignon," he says from his gooey state. His heat spike is waning. This might be the last time until his full heat takes over. We need to pack up and leave soon.

"Yes, Monroe."

"My inner omega is very unhappy we haven't fucked as much as the other girls. He doesn't like it. That's why I was so upset before."

I suppress a smile.

"Where's Carmen? I want to make a rule change," he says and looks around until he spots her.

Tara giggles. A rule change?

"I'm here, Sweet Thing. What's the rule?"

"After we bond, no private sex for a while. We fuck altogether. With me. We're a pack, not a random group of people."

This is it, the reason he's so emotional and angry. Well, this, and his heat. We all look at each other. Since we formed the pack, we could never make a rule like this. We were escorts at the Pack House and took on clients. Then it was rare to get all five of us together. I was with Legs...then we wanted an omega, so fucking outside of the pack was encouraged.

But there has always been a feeling that that was temporary and we'd eventually get to be all together at one point.

Why not now?

Bonding is going to change us.

Maybe for our bleeding hearts, this is a good idea.

Carmen is watching me, then she watches each girl, finally she looks back at Monroe.

"I think that's a great new rule. All together. What do you all think?"

Everyone says yes, quickly, and with the same conviction.

"Ok, we will talk to Sepp about it when he wakes up from his coma on the couch. But I doubt he'll protest. Once we are bonded, and at least for a while, we only have sex when it's just us, all together."

Tara squeals and I join her. It's exciting! I can't help but think how close we will all get. How this is going to change us into one pack. One solid pack.

I remove the machine from Monroe's cock, then lay over top of him. He wraps his arms around me.

"I love you so much. I love all of you. Wake up Sepp. I want to bond."

I huff out a laugh. We need to let the man rest. Then we will go to their place. Monroe can nest for real, and then we will be together forever.

Sepp bit Tara first.

He made his mark on her shoulder. Monroe and her made out for an hour afterwards. It was beautiful to watch. Then Sepp and Monroe fucked Honey together, at the same time, both men inside her cunt, while Sepp bit the top of her breast, and the three of them climaxed simultaneously.

Carmen was next, and Sepp fucked her while she laid on her side, and was able to get his teeth into her ass by curling his body over.

Lucy wanted a more dominant position, so she was on top, and offered Sepp her palm.

After, she slapped him with it.

He loved it.

Finally, it was my turn, and Sepp and I made love for a long time before he brought me into his pack with a bonding bite. He bit my wrist. What a joy to be claimed by someone I knew and already trusted.

A bond is so out of this world.

It's like I always knew what my Stars were thinking and feeling, but suddenly, I realized I was right. Without even looking at them, I could tell they were happy. And for the first time in my life, I was too.

Acknowledgements

I lost my job at the beginning of 2026. I'm a single mom with two teen daughters, and I'm the sole-provider, so you can imagine the situation I faced with unemployment. As scary as it was, what obscured everything was relief. I want to write. Every day, I'd fight for more time to write, so this was my time to get to do that. It's now halfway through the year, and I am still applying for jobs, interviewing at countless companies, but also just writing.

I wrote Knotorious Omega and then, when it was waiting for the scheduled time with the editor, I wrote this novella—Pack Star.

I wanted to write something quick, dirty, and fun to appease my lovely and veracious readers. This is a sweet treat just for you. A happy ending for Pack Star. I want to thank Thea for reading Cash City and making me feel like I'm good at this. I want to thank my betas Jessica, Luna, and Perri for giving me great insight. My ARC readers for understanding the vision. I want to thank Lanae for providing a beautiful and thorough edit. Tina for giving me a "WLW discount" on the cover, which made this all possible. Tina, you killed this cover. Finally, I want to thank my Substack subs: Cassie, Juanita, Mars, Readsalot81, Samantha, Jessica, and Zara. Thank you for your support—I am made whole by you.

xxx Shasta

About the Author

Shasta has enthralled readers with her unique writing style and penchant for high-stakes tension. What she is most known for is her well-written and intense spicy scenes, bringing the action to life in the most toe-curling way. She started out as a Kindle Vella author and then moved to indie publishing. She got her Bachelor of Arts in Literature from a liberal arts college in northern Utah, where she served as editor of the literary magazine for three years. She lives in Salt Lake City, UT, with her two kids and three cats. She has 100 more books to write, so stick around to read more steamy romance from her.

www.shastadeleon.com

Want More?

My next big release is Knotorious Omega, a stand-alone omegaverse suspense about a femme fatale and a private detective.

Knotorious Omega

Pre order now

Get Involved

Join Shasta's Substack to be signed up for her newsletter

https://substack.com/@lafemmeomegaverse

Shasta is most active these days on Instagram. Reach out and say hi!

https://www.instagram.com/lafemmeomegaverse/

Also by Shasta